Alma Fritchley was born [...] town in Nottinghamshire [...] Manchester area for the la[...] author of *Chicken Run* (The Women's Press, 1997) and *Chicken Feed* (The Women's Press, 1998), the first two Letty Campbell mysteries.

Also by Alma Fritchley from The Women's Press:

Chicken Run (1997)
Chicken Feed (1998)

ALMA FRITCHLEY
CHICKEN OUT

THE THIRD LETTY CAMPBELL MYSTERY

First published by The Women's Press Ltd, 1999
A member of the Namara Group
34 Great Sutton Street, London EC1V 0LQ

British Library Cataloguing-in-Publication Data
A catalogue record for this book is available from the British Library.

ISBN 0 7043 4619 2

Typeset in 11/12pt Plantin by FSH Ltd, London
Printed and bound in Great Britain by Cox & Wyman Ltd,
Reading, Berkshire

This book is dedicated to David and Anne Fritchley.
And Inland Revenue staff – everywhere.

Acknowledgements

Though not wishing to sound like an Emmy Award winner, I would like to thank the following 'Usual Suspects':

Eileen, for support and cheerfulness above and beyond the call of duty.

Gail, Julie, Pat, Brenda and Fran; where would I be without you?

Carole, for introducing me to goodies I may otherwise have missed and thanks to Tony and Dave for the hours of research.

Thanks also to AnneMarie and Yvonne, ready with a pint when I needed one!

Cheers to all those computer buffs who helped me find my way around my machine.

And very special thanks to Kirsty Dunseath for getting the joke.

Chapter 1

The funeral was so final and so bizarre that even the most heartbroken of relatives would wish it was over. I was beginning to wonder why I'd gone in the first place, and then I remembered it was the deceased's express wish that I organise the damned event. So I was honour-bound to attend.

What a palaver it had all been. It's not as though we had any blood ties. Our neighbouring farms were a tentative link at best. But somehow I'd managed to rake in the last of his line and, though they were a bit thin on the ground, George Norman Edward Evershaw did not leave this world unmourned.

My lover, Anne, had reluctantly agreed to help when my stress levels became more than she could bear. And her expertise as chief researcher at the library and noted author of historical tomes had paid dividends, as had a cleverly worded ad in the local paper, the *Calderton Echo*. If there was a sniff of money, any Evershaw with a vague connection to George was in the hunt.

As a chicken farmer, the role I'd taken of funeral

1

director was a surprising one. The Co-op would only ever contact me with regards to egg production. Solemnity and last rites did not sit well with my overalls and noisy livestock. But it was George himself who had approached me some months before his not unexpected death.

Gazing out of the kitchen window, I'd spotted his familiar figure trudging across my farmyard, scattering hens in his wake. That afternoon I'd been forced into doing a spot of baby-sitting for Anne's niece, Anna-Maria. Andy, her confidant and one-time boyfriend was the usual baby-sitter, but he had escaped for the day. I'd taken a break when Liam, eighteen months old and equally demanding as his headstrong mother, had fallen asleep in his playpen. Endearingly, he clutched a Sindy doll in one hand and a 'Nuke 'em till they drop' repeater ray gun in the other. He played constantly changing variations of 'Sindy Rules the World'. I'd been playing too that particular afternoon and I could have happily curled up in the playpen with him.

George stomped over the farm's threshold without a word. I had no idea how old he was but every wrinkle told a not very edifying story on that crazy-paving face. He waited until I'd presented him with a cup of tea before he spoke.

'Letty,' he began in his Ancient Mariner's voice. 'It's about my funeral.'

It transpired that George, rather dangerously, had been reading the *Independent* again. It always gave him ideas, and the latest fad for pre-death arrangements had appealed to the darker side of his soul. A special 10 per cent discount at the Co-op funeral parlour (for one month only) had been the final persuader.

'It's our Mary's lass I'd especially like to come,' he'd said over his brew. Gruffly he admitted that Stephanie, his late sister's daughter, was the last of the immediate line. 'But I don't know where she is exactly. Last I 'eard she was in Manchester at art college or summat. She kept the Evershaw name though,' he added reluctantly acknowledging that his sister, who'd left Calderton for a very different life in London (and briefly, Derbyshire), had never wed.

In a village such as Calderton, here in the heart of West Yorkshire, that was a very big deal indeed – well, it had been nearly forty years ago. Now the village was beginning to change with the times. Sky dishes had sprung up like so many woks in a Chinese takeaway and, with the advent of the MTV generation, a few prejudices had also fallen by the wayside. Though I was a relative newcomer to the area, happily my tendencies hadn't resulted in a burning at the stake. Even Anne, Calderton born and bred, had found a grudging acceptance. My friend Mrs Buckham, who runs the local store, reckoned Anne's comparatively recent admission to the Sapphic Sisterhood was because of 'all those books'.

'It's bound to take its toll,' she'd said ominously one afternoon over the produce-filled counter. 'Reading changes lives,' she'd confided (though Mrs Buckham had always preferred her entertainment to come from a box in the corner of her room).

I'd told the shopkeeper about George's morbid scheme and she'd sniffed her disapproval. 'He's always been a bit strange,' she said, ushering me into the back parlour. The hotter the gossip, the more inclined she was to invite me into the comfort of her home. 'If I'm needed, the customers will just have to ring the bell. Anyway, we're closer to the teapot in here as well as to God,' she chortled, referring to her new interest. C of E was out, according to Mrs Buckham, after watching a *Discovery* programme on Sky. Now bronze statues of Buddha stood elbow to elbow with images of little baby Jesus.

Even Ganesh the Indian elephant god could be seen on the overcrowded mantelpiece, his many trunked form giving Krishna, resplendent in blue, a run for his money. When Mrs Buckham mentioned God, she meant all of them.

Sylvia Buckham was probably five years George's junior, though she called him, alternately, 'the old man' or, more commonly, 'the old fool'. 'It's not surprising he never married,' she confided over the tea. I leaned forward, as she'd chosen to use her 'gossip whisper'. 'He's so mean, nobody would have him.' Her main concern was his will. 'He's hardly ever spent a bean. He'll have pots of money stashed somewhere.' She pondered on the unlikely event that George would leave her all his loot. 'You mark my words,' she went on, patting her full head of grey hair. 'Someone will do very well out of him.'

The post-funeral celebrations eventually proved that she was right.

Chapter 2

Despite George's premonitions, it was some months before anyone had to start digging a hole. Life carried on as normal, or as normal as it ever is in Calderton, and George survived another winter. His belief that some terrible disease would strike him down was unfounded. He met his maker in a way that no one could ever have predicted.

Calderton has one pub and at the time of George's sad demise a middle-aged couple from Bradford were running the show (or ruining the show; viewpoints are important here).

Not known for its innovative ideas, the local brewery (famous only for its Watmoughs Special Anti-Gravity Bitter*) had decided that the Frog and Bucket needed a shake-up. Usually that meant painting the ladies either a sickly pink or a putrid green and mopping the tap-room floor more than once a fortnight. But this time Watmoughs had something big in mind. In a move unknown in these parts the brewery had head-hunted

---

*Copyright by kind permission.

the Bradford Two and given them *carte blanche* to improve the centuries-old pub.

The young stud who had become director of the brewery after his father's death decided it was time to expand his market to include the commuter-belt yuppies who littered the area. The Frog and Bucket was to be the flagship of the brewery. Well, that was the theory anyway.

Mine hosts, John and Hilda Ramsbottom, did their best, but with the locals wary of any fresh ideas, suspicion hounded their every move. She was big-bosomed, blonde and Tenerife-tanned; he was slim, slick and thought he could sing. That was when the 'K' word was first uttered. Karaoke, the Japanese invention that convinced a whole nation it could carry a tune. From that moment it was obvious to everybody that the clientele Watmoughs hoped to encourage would not be forthcoming, though surprisingly the locals seized upon it as a kind of new invention of their own.

The opening night (and sadly George's last day on this earth) saw a packed and very mixed crowd. It was an occasion no one was likely to forget.

Chapter 3

Anne and I had been together just shy of six years and only our different lifestyles had stopped us from turning into a pair of old slippers. My partner was a librarian for most of her adult life, though a side-line in world travel (courtesy of her publisher) had shattered any tendency for convention and sometimes even normality. My chickens, my friends, and AnnaMaria and her young son (who both lived in the airy and roomy farmhouse attic) kept me sharp. Especially my friends. And one in particular. Julia, an ex-lover, has tenaciously pursued me since our break-up more than eight years ago. Not that she pursues me in the biblical sense. Sita, her partner and Labour MP for Caldervale, wouldn't allow that. Julia is the joker in the pack rather than a spanner in the works, and she and I are inextricably linked. More so now than ever.

She threw her towel and her creaking bank account in with AnnaMaria's savings and technical expertise to start a small local garage. According to Julia, they lurch from one financial crisis to another, though AnnaMaria confided to me that they are doing very well at the moment, thank you. Occasionally, wads of *lire* are flung at them from Julia's wealthy and doting Italian parents. Anne just about coped with Julia's larger-than-life presence. Julia lived in Manchester and it was rare for them both to be around the farm at the same time. This particular summer was proving to be an exception.

It was hot, it was Friday (though working on a farm, days tend to run into one another) and there was a buzz about the place that even the chickens could sense. I'd been doing some slow and not very productive work in the rock-hard soil of the garden. The spuds were wilting in the drought-like conditions, though the weeds thrived. Not that I cared particularly. Boiled and mashed, the concoction would be enjoyed by the hens whether the vegetables won the county's 'Perfect Potato' competition or not.

Sweat poured from my face as I put the hoe, spade and other garden paraphernalia back in the garage. As I pulled my straw hat from my head, my hair clung unpleasantly to my damp face. I'd managed to grow it into a short bob just as Julia, my fashion victim of a friend, assured me it was going out of style. Still, Anne liked it.

'No more butch in the streets and femme in the sheets.' She'd used the familiar phrase to tease me when finally, almost a year before, it had reached the required length. 'Now everyone knows how girlie you really are.'

We'd spent the afternoon in bed after that comment just to prove she was right.

Anyway, that night was to be the grand opening of the revamped Frog and Bucket and I was determined to make an effort. A good scrub-down wouldn't be a bad start and I headed indoors to remove the muck of the day.

The reopening of the Frog and Bucket was Calderton's cultural contribution to the twenty-first century.

Manchester had got a new stadium, a theatre and, courtesy of a terrorist bomb, a revamped and renewed city centre. We were happy with the boozer.

For years it had been the Dog and Partridge, until a fire gutted the place. When the insurance company finally coughed-up, the brewery refurbished and renamed the pub, the Packhorse. That was in the very late Seventies and for years the pub wallowed in a kind of limbo. The browns and creams of the era outstayed their welcome, as did the alcoholic landlord, who managed to drink the pub into debt until he was ousted five years ago. We'd had plastic tack since then – that is, until the pub finally hit the electronic age.

Several bombshells were dropped the day the pub reopened. AnnaMaria, with an appalling sense of timing, lit the first fuse.

My inherited farm had become a busy family home and, with Liam's arrival, baby chaos filled every corner. Toys littered the floor and clothes for washing, clothes for drying, clothes for ironing presented a hazard at every turn. AnnaMaria's dwelling in the attic had encroached upon the entire house. I'd learned to live with it and Anne, working frantically in the spare bedroom on her new book, *The Millennium: From Here to Eternity*, didn't even notice. But that was all to change.

'I had a phone call today,' AnnaMaria said rather matter of factly, as she stirred a pan of soup on the Aga.

Liam, proving the old adage about the 'terrible twos', screamed for attention in his playpen. Cricket commentary from Radio Five Live competed with the noise. Tiredly I had a game of 'Who Can Pull the Most Horrible Face' with the little boy. Liam's screams turned into shrieks. I didn't know which was worse.

'I said, I got a phone call today,' the soup stirrer announced loudly. She turned to face me. Her blonde

Björk-style hair gave her a look of constant surprise. I'd always preferred her crew cut myself.

I asked the required question. 'Who from?'

She turned back to the stove. 'Julia's mum.'

I was surprised. Religious festivals, birthdays and Independent Financial Advice were usually her reasons for contact. I checked my memory bank: no birthdays approaching, no major saint's days in the offing.

'What did she want?' I yelled over Liam's expanding lungs.

AnnaMaria mumbled something into the dinner. I switched the radio off – one less factor to contend with. Even Liam quieted. Perhaps he didn't like cricket. 'What did she want?' I repeated into an unusual and spooky silence.

AnnaMaria faced me again. I could hear the plop-plop of soup exploding behind her. 'She wants us to visit.'

'Who?' I asked stupidly.

'Sophia,' AnnaMaria sighed. 'She wants me to visit her in Milan.'

'That's fantastic,' I said, and meant it. 'You've not been away for ages.'

The last trip abroad had been a family affair, an extravagant celebration to mark the arrival of my big Four 0. AnnaMaria, the baby, me, Julia, Sita and even a reluctant Anne had all piled off to Amsterdam for three days. Talk about a lost weekend. AnnaMaria, with baby in tow, had done the cultural thing with Sita (who was far too respectable lately to do anything else), while the rest of us had hit the bars. I'd go into detail but I can't remember much about it.

'Do you want some of this?' she asked, spooning the thick home-made tomato soup into a bowl.

I realised I'd have to redecorate when Liam got his hands on the stuff.

'Please,' I said, suddenly hungry. 'Anyway, come on,

tell me about this phone call.'

I eased Liam out of his playpen and wrestled him into his high chair. I took a seat at the far end of the pine table. Even with his mother around, he still needed considerable help with hand-to-mouth co-ordination. The soup was gorgeous and Liam wore his well.

'Julia's mum wants us to go over for a holiday,' AnnaMaria explained. 'Just me and Liam.'

'Mmm, that's going to make you popular,' I muttered.

Julia would explode. She'd nearly had a nervous breakdown when AnnaMaria took maternity leave. Andy, still painfully fond of his ex-partner, had stepped into the mechanical breach, but to be honest I'd seen faster snails.

'I don't care. She can fuck off.'

AnnaMaria and Julia had an odd and rather delicate relationship. Secretly they were very fond of each other, but neither would ever admit it.

'Fuck!' Liam screamed happily. His spoon went flying.

'Don't make a mess,' AnnaMaria said rather too late. She chose to ignore the expletive.

'So you'll go then?'

'Of course,' she said, reaching for Liam's abandoned cutlery.

'It's too good an opportunity to miss. I've already asked Andy to help out. Anyway, you know how Sophia adores Liam. He'll have a great time.'

I looked across at the little boy. He didn't seem particularly adorable at that moment. In fact, he looked as though he'd had a nasty run-in with a lawn mower.

'So when do you go?' I asked carefully.

'Tuesday.'

'Next Tuesday?'

AnnaMaria nodded. 'Sophia's left tickets for me at the airport.'

Her relationship with Julia's mother had blossomed

with Liam's birth. Julia was an only child and at forty-odd she wasn't in the best position to start having children of her own. My own mother was in the same predicament as Sophia. For a non-related bunch, the family ties were very strong.

'Tuesday's a bit soon,' I tentatively suggested.

AnnaMaria plunged bread into her soup and shrugged before taking a bite. 'I've got passports, tickets and enough money. What's the problem?'

'You mean apart from Julia?' I smiled.

'She's just jealous,' AnnaMaria stated. She verbally ticked off possible problems one by one. 'The garage is sorted. The books are up to date. We've had this month's deliveries.' She paused. 'Do you know, I had to stop her from bidding for an Aston Martin at the last auction. The woman's mad, can you imagine how much it would cost, even just for an exhaust on a car like that?'

I shook my head. I had no idea.

'Well, a lot, believe me.'

'So what did you get?'

I'd not visited their forecourt for a while and occasionally something other than a bland Ford or Vauxhall made an appearance.

'An MG Midget,' she said, eyes lighting up.

The back door suddenly burst open and Julia stepped into the kitchen. 'Not any more,' she crowed. 'I've just sold it.'

'For the asking price?' AnnaMaria wanted to know.

'Oh yes, no problem. She didn't even quibble.'

The saleswoman preened like a bullfighter who'd just cornered her prey. Julia was following in her mother's footsteps and improving with age. Like an older and more confident Tanita Tikaram, she positively gleamed, and her black hair and olive skin put her up there as one of the more gorgeous women I had ever met. Her broad shoulders and inherited sense of style were enhanced by

12

clothes that someone in her line of work had no right to own. It's not surprising the taxman was always sniffing around.

'My God!' Julia said suddenly. 'What's wrong with Liam?'

'Tomato soup,' I explained.

She pulled a tissue from her pocket and wiped him down. A face appeared from beneath the red slime.

'Poor Liam, what sort of mother have you got?' she asked loudly.

Normally a row would have ensued, but AnnaMaria wisely kept quiet. She managed a snappy, 'Why are you here anyway?'

Julia took a moment to help herself to the remains of Liam's tea, then, 'It is half-past five,' she said. 'What do you want me to do? Work nights?'

AnnaMaria cleared the table noisily. 'I thought you were seeing Sita about the thing tonight.'

'I rang her,' Julia explained. 'She agreed to do the pub's official opening, but she can't stay for long. She's got to get to London for a meeting of her Parliamentary subcommittee. Something about this art thing. I probably won't see her for weeks,' she grumbled.

'Art thing? Julia, what are you on about?' AnnaMaria asked.

Julia was suddenly irritable, probably from hunger. If she didn't eat every four hours her sugar and tolerance levels plummeted.

'You know, to do with the Swiss,' she answered abruptly. 'The art treasures and gold stolen from the Jews during the war. It's been all over the news for the past God-knows-how-long.'

Julia wasn't exactly your *News at Ten* type. Channel Five soundbites and Kirsty Young's deep-throated delivery had been designed for her.

'Is that supposed to be an explanation?' AnnaMaria

went on in a tight voice as a mask of boredom slipped over her face.

I'm sure a similar one descended over mine. We'd been subjected to Sita's Parliamentary subcommittees before and watching paint dry would be an exciting Olympic sport by comparison.

Sita Joshi was still an MP by the skin of her teeth. Controversy had dogged every career move she'd ever made, though as a former actress she'd acquired the necessary experience for the backbiting that went on in British politics. She was an exceptional woman and, despite a few personal clangers dropped in the past, an effective vote catcher. She appealed to a vast cross-section of the electorate. It was just a shame they didn't all live in the same area. Second-and third-generation British Asian women flocked to her. And as an out MP, lesbians adored her. But still the leadership dithered. Overlooked as a candidate at the last local elections for the risky and challenging Manchester constituency she craved, she'd been left with Caldervale, a safer low-key seat that a mad axeman could hold onto as long as he was a Labour supporter. I was never sure whether it was despite or because of Sita's nature that she kept her job, but so far she was doing the business.

She'd had quite an effect on Julia. For the moment my friend's 'tart with a heart' phase was over. Sita demanded loyalty and fidelity, and amazingly, knowing Julia's past, she was getting both. Despite their differences, culturally, financially and historically, they'd forged quite a partnership. The press had at first shown considerable interest in Sita and Julia, and the paparazzi had been a pain in the backside for a while, but eventually they found a more exciting couple to follow. Despite royal tragedies, Charles and Camilla were always going to make better copy.

'So Sita's doing the cutting of the ribbon, is she?' I asked.

'She said she might even give us a song if there's Bhangra on the juke box.'

'Karaoke machine,' AnnaMaria corrected her.

'Whatever,' Julia said airily. 'Anyway, what's this about you and Milan?'

'How the fuck did you know?' AnnaMaria asked, clearly surprised.

'Fuck, fuck, fuck,' Liam shrieked again.

God, we'd have Social Services round at this rate.

'Sshh, Liam,' Julia ordered.

'Come on,' AnnaMaria urged.

Julia sighed. 'I do still speak to my mother, you know. We occasionally have a conversation.'

'And she told you?'

'Yes.'

'And you don't mind?'

Julia sighed again. 'No.'

AnnaMaria was suspicious. 'What about the garage?'

'What about it?'

'You're not worried?'

'Should I be?' Julia countered.

AnnaMaria, for one amazing moment, was lost for words. It was obvious she'd been preparing for battle all day, but the war had been won without a shot being fired.

'I'll go and sort some washing then,' AnnaMaria mumbled, and she grabbed a burbling Liam and headed upstairs.

Julia grinned at me. 'That was easy.'

'You're up to something, I always know,' I replied warily.

Anne was my partner and I loved her dearly, but even so Julia (sometimes as clear as glass) was much easier to fathom. The grin widened. Those pearly teeth were the only things that prevented her tongue from flapping. 'Go and see Anne,' she suggested finally. 'Go on, she'll explain,' and she waved me towards the stairs.

'You dry the pots then,' I ordered, and flung my

favourite 'Greetings from Skegness' tea towel in Julia's direction. The towel was from my mother, currently revisiting her childhood on the east coast: Billy Butlin, a bittersweet memory of years gone by.

I followed the fizzing noise coming from Anne's laser printer *in situ* in the spare bedroom. I found Anne asleep across the computer. The soup AnnaMaria had left earlier was stone cold by her side.

Her manuscript towered on either side of her. If *The Millennium: blah, blah, blah* got any bigger, she'd still be reviewing it when the next one rolled by. I gave her silent form a gentle nudge and her reading glasses clattered to the floor. She'd changed her working hours lately. Promotion and a transfer from the local library to the main one in Halifax had given her greater flexibility with her hours. Nine to five had been exchanged for seven to twelve giving her more time with her computer but, sadly, no more time with me. The trouble was, she'd exchanged one job for two and we found ourselves spending less and less time together. Promotional tours didn't help either, but she wanted to grasp all the opportunities while she could. Her style of non-fiction would have only a short life-span, or so she thought during her darker moments. Even if she was right, though I doubted it, I didn't want her to drop dead of exhaustion.

She opened one eye to peer at me and gave me a smile that eclipsed anything Julia could come up with. Her hair, newly dyed dark brown, was devoid of the grey streaks I'd become accustomed to.

'It looks better on the book cover,' she'd said with a smile. 'It stops me looking ancient.'

Panic had set in as the years flashed by, and with an important birthday not so very far way as well, she'd had the hair job and had hastily installed a cycling machine at the end of our bed. She used it too. Only the previous week she'd boasted that she'd just hit a thousand miles. Her muscular knees were proof of that. But sprawled across her workstation, she looked as though she could barely draw breath, never mind indulge in excessive cardiovascular exercise.

The smile suddenly broadened. 'It's finished,' she breathed.

'What?' I asked, knowing anyway.

'The book, silly.' She raised her head – radiant is too bland a word to describe her expression. 'It needs editing and I still need a conclusion, some sort of final chapter will do, but basically, *voilà*!' She tapped the piles of paper emphatically.

'Do I get a mention?' I asked, hoping my earlier, selfish feelings of neglect would now be behind me.

She smiled but didn't answer and instead rubbed her tired eyes with the heel of her hand. 'God, I'm starving. I don't think I've eaten all day.'

Over the last few months I'd found that with literary aspiration came forgetfulness...

Chapter 4

Sita arrived about seven-thirty and opted to wait for Julia in the lounge, the only quiet room in the house. She'd abandoned her usual safe and severe work suit and instead wore something comfortable in cashmere.

Half of Julia's wardrobe had ended up at the farm since her working relationship with AnnaMaria had begun and, finding no reason to go home, she used all the hot water and changing facilities to make herself ready. Female members of the household ran around in various stages of undress. As a last resort I'd drawn the kitchen curtains, boiled a kettle and had a wash at the sink. Something my gran used to do some thirty-odd years ago. Doubting that the brewery had installed air-conditioning and anticipating a hot and damp night, I opted for cool and baggy cotton pants and a colourful T-shirt that disguised my less than voluptuous figure.

The pub was a twenty-minute walk away and Sita, needing to be there ahead of time, drove off early in her unmistakable red Saab 900i, taking Julia with her.

'So what's your news then?' I asked Anne as we left the

house. The air was still and warm, a perfect summer's evening. Short days and cold nights seemed a long way off.

'I don't think you're going to like the executive decision I've made,' Anne said, clutching my arm.

I could feel her ribs beneath her short-sleeved blouse. I started to plan menus.

'You're not going away again?' I moaned. Spring had seen her travelling to a women's book fair in Paris with only her agent for company. Spring, Paris and women were three words I didn't care for.

'No, nothing planned for a while yet. No, it's Julia.'

'What's she done now?'

'Well, it's not so much what she's done, it's what she wants to do.'

Anne waited while I prompted her. 'And?' I asked.

'She's going to be staying here till September.'

My stomach gave a sudden lurch. Julia made Liam look well behaved.

'Oh no,' I managed.

'Oh yes' Anne laughed.

I didn't know why she was finding it so funny. The two women were never likely to audition for *Friends*. Julia could find trouble in a Morecambe tearoom. Her life had progressed counter to the norms of others'. Instead of running smoothly with the odd hitch, Julia had followed the line of most resistance. Trauma and trouble were succeeded by a quiet but short-lived peace. I should know, I'd lived with her long enough.

'Two things,' I said finally. 'Why does she want to stay, but more importantly, why don't you mind?'

Anne slipped her arm from mine and her bony hip ground against my thigh. Linda McCartney's vegetable cutlets, chips, peas and gravy for tea tomorrow, I decided.

'Well, she's renting out her flat for one thing.'

'Oh?'

'And with AnnaMaria and Liam going away, it seemed the perfect opportunity.'

'For what?'

'To stay at the farm with us.'

'You still haven't explained why,' I said, exasperated. I could tell Anne was beginning to enjoy this cat-and-mouse exchange.

'You know the GMex conference centre is hosting the World Ladies' Darts Tournament?'

I didn't, and I had no idea what this was leading to, but I wasn't about to admit it. 'Mmm,' I said non-committally.

Anne began kicking a stone along the dry path with the edge of her sandal. Thanks to World Cup fever still gripping the nation, she had rediscovered her love of football, though I doubted she was about to be signed up for the England squad. Even so it was nice to see her more her usual self: less stressed, more time for me.

'Well,' she went on. 'A couple of her friends have qualified and they've nowhere to stay.' Somehow the conversation got even more unlikely. 'They're friends she met at college apparently.' Anne let fly with the cobble and it crashed into a nearby hedge. One-nil to England.

'Hang on,' I said, before she imagined herself through to the World Cup final. 'You're telling me Julia's got friends in the darts world?'

'Yep.' She laughed. 'Amazing, isn't it?'

'And she met them at college?'

Her laughs got louder.

'*That* college?' I pressed.

She nodded, eyes dancing. We both knew of Julia's privileged education. Even your average royal would have been envious of Julia's start in life. And to think her posh college (a finishing school really) in Switzerland would have spawned world-class darts players was really too much. I shook my head in wonder.

'She's not *sleeping* with them, is she?'

Anne snorted through her laughter. 'As if Sita would let her!'

'So what's the story then?'

'According to Julia, all is as it seems. No hidden agendas, no shady deals. Just friends staying over.'

'Friends staying over, my backside!' I paused. 'And they play darts for a living?' I asked, incredulous.

'Apparently,' Anne said, laughter turning to howls.

After months in front of a computer, she was ready to spread her wings a little. And Julia's performances were enough to set anybody off. A sudden feeling of elation hit me. If Anne was her old self, perhaps our relationship would get back to normal too.

'I'm sure she'll tell you all about it. She just wanted to clear the way with me first. She knows she can always twist you round her little finger.'

'That is so untrue!' I choked and I made a grab for Anne.

She cleverly avoided my grasp. After six years, she knew every move I was about to make. Muscular knees pumping, she took off down the path. Ryan Giggs couldn't have kept up with her, so I didn't even try.

'I'll get you,' I yelled, creaking after her, though I knew I never would.

Chapter 5

Every local within a ten-mile radius was at the Frog and
Bucket. A wider cross-section of humanity had never
assembled under one roof. Sylvia Buckham and her
friend Amna from the cash-and-carry were there,
propping up a beribboned and as yet unopened bar,
though a whisky and an orange juice respectively stood
before the two women. Amna's daughter, Jabeen,
twenty-one, bright and a would-be politician, hung onto
Sita's every word. Julia hovered close by.

Andy, having taken the first shift in the pub
(AnnaMaria would swap baby-sitting duties with him
later), gave me a small and silent wave of acknowledgement. Other neighbours greeted me, including George,
and, apart from Julia, there wasn't a yuppie in sight.

The karaoke machine, also bound with a red ribbon,
glowed like a revamped Tardis next to the bar. John
Ramsbottom was excitedly taking orders from would-be
Sinatras and Basseys. The chalked-up running order was
growing fast. Sita's name, not surprisingly, wasn't among
the artistes. George had taken second slot after the

landlord, and sixth, and eighth. I knew that, by the eighth, he wouldn't even be able to remember his own name, never mind focus on the words on screen. John, happily adding another name to the list, obviously didn't know him as well as I did.

We made our way over to spare seats by Andy and it was a moment before I realised there was something odd underfoot. A carpet. And one that I didn't stick to with every step. My God, the brewery really had gone to town.

We sat down and the din of thirsty pub-goers suddenly quieted – a bit like Liam or the chickens when feeding time came round. Hilda Ramsbottom, gin-flushed cheeks glowing, appeared behind the bar with a pair of oversized plastic scissors clutched in one hand.

'Ladies and gentlemen,' she bellowed. 'And Mrs Joshi.' She almost curtsied. 'Welcome to the Frog and Bucket.' Her next words were a guarantee of the pub's instant success: 'The first round is on the house.'

Managing to restrain themselves, the locals didn't flock to the bar.

'But first, Mrs Joshi, if you could do the honours?'

The MP resisted the temptation to utter a few words herself and, as Julia looked on in amusement, merely smiled for the camera (Mrs Buckham's niece, Janice, recording this historical moment for the local rag) and snipped the ribbon with the child-proof scissors.

Cheers all round and then the rush to the bar. John cranked up the karaoke machine and we were off.

By eleven all those who'd hoped to be drunk already were. We didn't know it, but George was probably dead by then. He was already drunk by the time we arrived at the pub, so you can imagine what state he must have been in by the time he staggered out to catch the off-licence before it closed at nine. Unknown to the brewery, it wasn't unusual for his poacher's jacket to conceal more than the odd dead pheasant. What was unusual, an hour or so later, was the arrival of a stranger; a dark-haired, loose-limbed creature had slipped into our midst.

She had been subjected to the sort of scrutiny usually reserved for cat-walk androgyne, though she was somewhat older than the average superwaif. Green-eyed and gorgeous, she couldn't fail to arouse our interest. Though perhaps that had been her intention.

Demi Moore, I'd thought, with a sudden unhealthy and drunken interest, before Californian craziness got the better of her.

'Dyke,' Julia muttered under her breath.

'One of yours?' Mrs Buckham asked, with un-accustomed reserve.

After a while it became obvious to anyone familiar with film noir that this woman was casing the joint. Even Julia, alone after waving Sita off hours before, overcame her usual physical interest long enough to notice that.

John Ramsbottom was blissfully unaware of two things: the stranger's close examination of the place and any musical connection his rendition of 'New York, New York' may once have had. His wife, on the other hand, missed nothing. The fact that the woman hadn't bought a drink, not even a glass of coke, was the main cause for concern. Sadly, the stranger had left before she could be challenged. Over the years, there wasn't much that hadn't been tolerated, but not buying a drink was a mortal sin.

By this time, though, our gang of four were well into our cups, and the attractive stranger's arrival was a quickly forgotten blip in the evening's entertainment.

Only events at a later date would serve to remind us.

Chapter 6

The following morning brought a well-deserved hang-over and a vague and warm memory of the previous night's events. I was startled to find myself fully dressed, even down to my dusty boots. Recollection of an egg-gathering round conducted at about three in the morning flittered around my consciousness. Half a dozen shit-splattered eggs balanced precariously in one of Anne's shoes confirmed my suspicions. I tentatively turned to my lover, who was naked except for the reading glasses perched at the end of her nose. A trashy lesbian novel lay near at hand across the duvet.

The metal arms of her glasses were bent slightly out of shape. Was that due to sex, I wondered, waiting for an erotic memory. But no, she had been too tired, and I'd been too drunk. I dimly recalled her less than gentle rejection of me, but a safety mechanism somewhere in the back of my brain thankfully clouded that particular memory, though not quickly enough to numb one small arrow of pain.

I shook my head to dispel the feeling and risked a

glance at the clock. Eight-thirty. Why was the world so silent? Hens should have been breaking down the bedroom door by now, demanding food and attention. And if not the hens, then where was Liam? Only the murmur of the early morning TV news echoed hollowly through the bedroom walls. AnnaMaria, I realised, rescuing me from my chores. I tried for more sleep. No chance. I examined Anne closely, her deep and even breaths showed no sign of altering rhythm. Her end-of-book celebrations had concluded with a bottle of champagne courtesy of Julia and she would be lost to us all for a while yet.

Despite the promising start to the evening, I had an unpleasant feeling she'd spoken to everyone but me. I slid quietly from the bed. The ceiling revolved once and I needed a moment to gather myself before I could tackle the bright cheeriness of the bathroom.

It wasn't until I'd cleared the fur ball from my mouth with Listerine that I began to feel whole again and put thoughts of Anne behind me. I took an immediate turn for the worse, though, when I hit the kitchen. Liam, sucking cornflakes, greeted me with a gurgle and the clatter of spoon against dish. I knew something was wrong when I spotted AnnaMaria ironing.

'What's up?' I asked, not really wanting an answer.

'I've got some bad news,' she said seriously.

'Oh?'

'Well, sad and bad,' she corrected. 'It's old George, he's dead.'

'Bloody hell! When? How?'

I was surprised as much as anything. He'd looked well enough the last time I'd seen him.

'He drowned.'

'Drowned?'

We were in the middle of a drought. The third one in as many summers. There wasn't a full reservoir (or a

26

decent puddle come to that) for miles.

Steam hissed hysterically from the iron as AnnaMaria attacked another item of clothing.

'Yeah,' she said. 'Drowned. In the bath.'

'George! In the . . .'

'Don't speak ill of the dead,' she snapped in a strangely old-fashioned way.

'His tin bath?' I pressed. 'Why would he bother with that huge thing at that time of the night?'

AnnaMaria gave me a look. 'No, upstairs, in the bathroom.'

'Since when has he used that?' I asked stumped.

My outburst wasn't so surprising. George had had his bathroom fitted when government grants were available for such things, though as far as I knew he'd never used it and had only had it fitted because it didn't cost him anything. He still had an outhouse, where the Victorian closet was situated, and, as for washing, well, the kitchen sink proved quite sufficient. For a more thorough going-over, he preferred the old tin bath that hung on the farm wall. He dragged it in a couple of times a year. 'Twenty kettles of water was plenty, and cheaper than putting the boiler on,' he'd confided over a drink one evening. 'It did for the dog as well,' he'd insisted.

Sadly, over the years I'd been witness on a few occasions to this unpleasant occurrence. Having no kitchen curtains in his windows, one mistimed glance and George's naked glory was there for all to see. I realised it was a problem I would never encounter again.

'So, sort of natural causes then?' I asked AnnaMaria.

'Well, early days yet,' she said slowly. 'The police are being a bit cagey. His death is "under investigation", according to the gossip. The police have been crawling over his house all morning,' she explained. 'I think they've gone now,' and she glanced out of the window, nodding to herself. 'There was a half-empty bottle of whisky clutched in his hand by all accounts,' she added with a slight smile.

'Half empty? George? Surely not?'

'He'll probably haunt us for the rest,' AnnaMaria mused.

I didn't ask her where she got such inside information; news like this was usually flashed from house to house before the corpse was even cool.

'So who reported it?'

I sat down at the kitchen table and helped myself to cereal. Liam shrieked for more and I quickly obliged. I was rewarded with a few moments' peace.

'That is the odd part,' AnnaMaria said, relinquishing the iron. 'Do you remember the woman in the pub last night?'

'No.'

She sighed. 'Come on, Letty, the one that Julia thought was gay. That skinny woman with the short hair. The landlady was moaning about her because she didn't buy a drink.'

I finally nodded, recalling the cropped dark hair and fine bone structure with a guilty jolt.

'Well,' she said, deep into the story, 'that was George's niece. The one you contacted ages ago for when, you know, George snuffed it.'

'Really?' I said, amazed. 'I've only spoken to her on the phone. My, hasn't she got a great sense of timing?'

I munched cornflakes, remembering, with some discomfort, the woman's impact on me.

'That's what I thought,' AnnaMaria said. 'But from what I've heard the police say, he'd been dead a couple of hours by the time she turned up.'

'Odd, eh?'

'Suspicious, if you ask me. Apparently there's to be a coroner's report.'

'Poor old George, and to top it all, being messed about with at his age.'

'Poor old coroner, you mean.' AnnaMaria chuckled bleakly. 'Still, at least he was clean.'

I spluttered on my breakfast. 'That's terrible! What happened to speaking ill of the dead?' I said, but couldn't help laughing.

The phone rang then (the first of many calls that day). It was Mrs Buckham, wanting the latest gossip and willing to impart some of her own in exchange.

I told her what I knew and, despite her 'oohing' and 'aahing' she was one step ahead of me already. 'There's a remembrance service tomorrow,' she confided. 'Our Janice is doing a piece in tonight's *Calderton Echo*. It's terrible about the, erm, hospital thing, isn't it?' she added with a whisper.

I thought a moment. Post-mortem she meant, though no one ever mentioned the word. Such goings-on were met with universal disapproval.

'Meddling,' she said. 'At his age. It's disgusting, abusing the dead like that.' She paused and suddenly let it slip why she was so well informed. 'Janice was up in the middle of the night. They needed pictures for the *Echo*. I bet George never thought his house would be on the front page one day,' Mrs Buckham mused. 'Covered in blood, it was.'

'The house?' I choked. 'I thought he drowned.'

I felt sick. A murder? In Calderton? NEXT DOOR TO ME? The ownership of a pair of Rottweilers and a set of new, state-of-the-art door locks was suddenly appealing.

'Who's to say?' Mrs Buckham blithely went on. 'The cupboard in his bedroom was in a right state. You know what his house was like. There wasn't a door hung straight. Every one poised at an angle to take your eye out if you weren't careful.'

'Sylvia, what are you saying?'

'I'm saying, and I've said it before, the police are

useless. All this fuss. Nothing was taken, you know, so they can't pin it on a robbery. Not that there was much to take,' she added with a sniff. 'Drunk, clumsy and stupid, that was George all over. Suspicious circumstances my eye. They'd be better off investigating that spate of robberies last year. Cleaned half of Calderton out and what did the police do? Nothing. No arrests, no suspects, nothing solved. They want sacking, the lot of them.'

This confused litany did nothing to ease my mind.

'I can see him now,' she went on. 'Staggering about, cracking his head a good one and then SPLAT!'

I yanked the phone away from my ear for a second at the force of her exclamation.

'Head first into the bath,' she finished on a slightly quieter note. The picture she painted was grossly unappealing, but feasible.

'Did he have his clothes on?' I asked, as a thought tugged at my mind.

'His long johns,' Mrs Buckham explained. 'I doubt if he ever took them off.'

Oh, but he did, Sylvia, he did.

I'd seen the grey one-piece undergarment hung on the line from time to time (well, maybe twice). Left over from his demob days, it was quite the most revolting item of clothing I'd ever clapped eyes on.

'There were rabbits in the bathroom,' Sylvia continued.

'Rabbits?'

'Yes, dead ones. I don't even want to think what he was doing with those.'

I couldn't begin to imagine.

She went on, suddenly excited, 'Sergeant Sam is due any minute. They'll want to know when I saw him last, what he said, what his mood was like and all that.'

Poor Sam. I could imagine the sort of earbashing he was in for.

'You'll be on his hit list as well. Tell them nothing,

Letty. Investigation? They couldn't investigate the plumbing.'

A police visit. I thought perhaps I'd go out for the day.

Suddenly events of a more financial nature took precedence over possible mysteries. 'Do you have to pay for this post-mortem?' Mrs Buckham enquired. 'Will it come out of the estate?'

I assured her it wouldn't. 'It's a legal thing,' I explained, though to be honest I was no wiser than Mrs Buckham. My clinical expertise tended to come from Channel Four's *ER* or *Chicago Hope*. The latest repeats of *Casualty* were way too realistic for me. 'I suppose with it being an unexpected death,' I added.

'Unexpected?' she shrieked down the phone. 'I've been expecting him to drop dead for the last twenty years, the way he drinks ... used to drink,' she corrected herself.

'Well, I'm going to ring the Co-op later. We've got other relatives to contact. Admittedly there aren't many,' I said. 'But Stephanie Evershaw is here already, as you know.'

'Mmm. Funny that. She was questioned early this morning. Had to give a statement.' Sylvia sniffed, annoyed she didn't know more. 'Did you get to meet her?'

'Only in passing,' I said.

'Anyway, if you need any advice, you know where I am.'

We said our goodbyes and I began to make other calls.

Chapter 7

The late edition of the local paper carried a small report on George's death, tastefully worded by Mrs Buckham's niece: 'Yesterday evening, the body of George Norman Edward Evershaw, late of EastBrook Farm, Calderton, was discovered at his home.' Unlike her aunt, Janice had chosen to use the dreaded words:

A post-mortem is being carried out and police sources say Mr Evershaw's death is under investigation. Several witnesses to his last moments have been asked to come forward for questioning. A remembrance service will be conducted at EastBrook Farm by Mr Evershaw's only surviving close relative, Stephanie Evershaw-Adam. The funeral will be held later in the week, the date to be confirmed.

Anne, recovering from the previous night, was reading over my shoulder. We were alone in the kitchen. Julia, against all odds, was helping AnnaMaria pack Liam's clothes for their forthcoming trip to Italy. I'd got used to the idea of Julia as a house guest for the summer, though she was under strict orders not to, well, not to do anything.

'Crikey, George dead. I thought he'd outlive us all.'

I gave her a quick run-down on the latest events. Her jaw dropped open in surprise and she took the paper from me for a closer look.

'Crikey,' she said again, after reading the report, then added in surprise, 'Oh, I didn't know his niece was married.'

'No, neither did I,' I said, noting the newly acquired double-barrelled name.

The phone rang; Mrs Buckham again.

'I've been wanting to ring you,' she said excitedly. 'She's married, you know.'

The phone crackled, static temporarily drowning out the shopkeeper's next words.

'SHE'S MARRIED,' she bellowed again.

'I GATHERED,' I yelled back.

Magically, the lines cleared as the summer storm that threatened in the distance suddenly lifted. It looked as though the long awaited downpour wasn't going to materialise.

There was a long pause as Mrs Buckham collected her thoughts.

'It's Evershaw-Adam now,' she confided, as if I didn't know. 'Janice says the husband's not local.'

'Oh?' I said.

'He's from down south...' she waited for an appropriate response.

'Really?' I managed.

'Derby. Though with a name like that, I don't suppose he's from there originally,' she muttered down her nose.

With geography lessons taken when Chamberlain was around, Mrs Buckham can be forgiven for losing her bearings, but even so, no stretch of the imagination could put Derby south of Watford.

'Claude,' Mrs Buckham continued.

'Sorry?'

'He's called Claude. Claude Evershaw-Adam.' It was obvious she disapproved of these married and hyphenated names, but not for the obvious reasons. She went on to explain why, in a conversation we'd had once before. 'It's not the Forties now, for goodness' sake,' she ploughed on. 'Do you know one in four, or is it three? Anyway, a lot of marriages end in divorce nowadays. Why can't they be like you gays and just live together?'

I'd tried to explain the growing penchant for gay marriages once, but she'd looked at me as if I'd gone raving mad.

She went on, 'In my day it was the done thing. Left school at fourteen, worked for a bit, started courting, got married, had children. And that was your lot. And what was that like? Miserable, that's what. You'd think people would learn, wouldn't you? My husband wasn't so bad, I suppose, but ooh, I wish I had my time again. I'd have done every college course going. And married? Pah,' she said dismissively. 'I'd've never washed a pair of underpants in my life given half a chance.' She paused in her wanderings down memory lane. 'He was ever so charming,' she said finally.

'Who?'

'Her husband, Claude. He was in the shop today. Buying cigars,' she added. 'And not just the Hamlets, either. Never thought I'd sell those Cuban things.' There was a hint of pride in her voice. 'You'll have to meet him,' she said. 'You probably will, at the remembrance service. Though how Stephanie Evershaw can – '

'Stephanie Evershaw-Adam,' I interrupted with a smile.

'Stephanie Evershaw-Adam then. How she can conduct George's remembrance service is beyond me.

She hardly knew him, never mind remember him.' Mrs Buckham suddenly brightened. 'And then we've got the will to look forward to,' she said. 'Never a dull moment here. Anyway, got to go, there's someone at the door. I'll see you at the farm tomorrow. Bye, Letty.'

The phone went dead.

'Sylvia?' Anne asked from behind the local paper.

'Who else?' I said, and went on to explain the short and strange conversation.

Anne chuckled. 'Claude, eh?' She put the paper down. 'Claude Adam, you say? Mmm, I know that name from somewhere. Oh, well. I'm sure it'll come back to me.'

Despite a village full of curious people who would kill for a crumb of gossip, Anne, with her book finished and idleness beckoning, was obviously in no rush to impart any information. A moment later she was back amidst the pages of the *Echo* and lost to the book review.

Somewhat at a loose end myself, I went upstairs to see if AnnaMaria needed a hand. She was already at Julia's throat when I climbed the wooden stairs that led to the attic's hatchway. I knocked for admission and a red-faced AnnaMaria flung it open angrily. Clambering over the wooden fence that surrounded the open hatch (an ingenious device that stopped an increasingly curious Liam from plummeting to his death), I took in the mess that littered the floor. There was barely a pause for breath before the two women were screaming at each other again. Julia, for once, had lost her rag.

'Of course he'll need some warm clothes, you silly bitch!' she yelled.

'Don't you call me a bitch!' AnnaMaria screeched back. 'Go and sort your hormones out, you fucking... oaf!' she managed.

'Oaf?'

Julia rose above the menopausal insult. 'It can get cold at night, remember. I don't see why my mother should buy him clothes just because you're too stupid to bring some with you.'

I could see that this was the crux of the problem. Julia, as AnnaMaria had predicted, was jealous.

Stung, AnnaMaria straightened. 'Give me the case, Julia.'

No movement from Julia.

She held her hand out. 'Give me the case,' she repeated through gritted teeth. 'GIVE ME THE FRIGGING CASE!'

Julia flung the article on the settee. 'Pack it yourself then,' she muttered. 'And don't you be late on Monday!' she yelled through the half-open bedroom door to Andy.

Completely untouched by the outburst, he waved an acknowledgement to Julia and went back to football-watching with Liam. I used to worry about the little boy's role models, but his favourite toy was still Sindy so I suppose that balanced things out a bit.

Julia, unoaf-like, slammed through the hatch and retreated to the main part of the house. Normally she would have just kept on walking, but her flat, overtaken by dart-wielding friends, was out of bounds.

She did leave by the front door though, and I watched her progress from the attic's dormer window. She barged into the greenhouse, pursued by ever hungry and ever hopeful chickens.

'What is it with you two?' I asked AnnaMaria quietly.

'Oh, she'll get over it,' she insisted, folding Liam's warm and woolly jumpers. She placed them neatly into the case. There didn't seem much point in making a comment.

'She can't bear it when her mum makes a fuss of me.'

She smiled to herself. Somehow she thought she was points ahead in some imaginary game they played. It was all too stressful for me. Anne and I rarely argued, and if we felt a niggle coming on, we'd go shopping. Our quality time together was far too precious (and too rare) to waste on rowing.

To divert painful thoughts I explained the latest in George's eternal progress.

'Do you reckon she's here for his dosh then?' AnnaMaria asked, then urged me to sit on Liam's case so she could close it.

'I don't know whether he's got any,' I said as she secured the fastenings.

''Course he's got some. He was always a tight-arse.' She laughed, having used her favourite form of insult. 'The farm alone must be worth a few quid.'

'Yeah, well, I'm sure the valuers will be here with the vultures before long.' I sighed. 'I wonder what sort of neighbours we'll get?'

That hadn't been a thought I'd dwelt on much. Though Anne had expressed some concern.

'They could turn it into anything,' she'd said shortly after hearing of his demise. 'It's hardly a listed building, is it?'

It needed condemning, not listing.

'Well, you can write and tell me all about it when I'm in Italy sunning myself,' AnnaMaria crowed.

'Don't worry,' I said, smiling. 'I'll keep you posted.'

Chapter 8

Gathered together the following day, we were the chosen few. An élite assembly of George Evershaw's earthly representatives, here to witness a eulogy which made him sound more like Nelson Mandela than the crusty old soak we knew. Judging by Mrs Buckham's reassessment of the deceased at any rate. By some miracle, George had been transformed overnight from a drunken old fool, 'and mean with it', to a vital and important member of the community.

Julia, who'd agreed to accompany me to the service (Anne found the whole thing too depressing – 'The funeral's bad enough,' she'd said – and AnnaMaria was simply 'unavailable'), listened to Mrs Buckham in amazement. Later, in the pub, we'd agreed that George's sudden exit had rattled the old woman.

'She's no spring chicken,' Julia pointed out brutally. 'She can feel Old Father Time nipping at her ankles.'

Julia, who would live for ever, had banished all thoughts of a time when she would be older. Bryan Adams's song 'Eighteen 'til I die' could have been written for her.

Thankfully, though, Sylvia Buckham hadn't been invited to add her comments during the service. Stephanie Evershaw-Adam's words were quite enough.

Now, one way and another, either through fielding posh clients during my insurance work years or via Julia's assortment of friends and foes, I'd encountered some pretty impressive women. And none more so than George's niece.

We'd arrived at my ex-neighbour's run-down farm just before midday. Already his old pals, such as they were, had gathered, along with Mrs Buckham and what few ageing and distant relatives I'd managed to find. They milled about the yard, most of them, memories fudged by the years, wondering why they were there at all. There was cousin Florence, who, despite her tiny form, was almost a Les Dawson clone, and her bored young step-grandson, Jack, who'd brought her down from Huddersfield for the day. A couple of others, whose names and connections I'd forgotten, chatted quietly by the long-disused pigsty. It was a sad but true fact that, in life, George had never commanded such interest. But today, with his sudden death still not explained, he was the centre of attention, overshadowed only perhaps by his surprisingly commandeering niece. George's farm was almost as familiar as my own, and it was a bit of a shock to find that, now the police had done everything they needed to and handed it back to his relatives, the place had already been gutted. Stephanie's doing, at a guess. Even the ancient lino had been ripped up, revealing cracked and hand-painted terracotta tiles with curious tramlines all over them. Laid in the Fifties, the lino, with its fading abstract pattern, was a must-have for memorabilia freaks.

I glanced around the bare old house. George's presence was disappearing fast. Chairs had been lined up along one grey and mildewed wall. Mismatched and oft-painted, the dining-room seats offered a last connection to my old neighbour. Opposite were two chairs of a more substantial nature, and the setting reminded me of the more horrendous interviews I'd been subjected to in the past. Quietly the dozen or so of us in attendance took our places and moments later Stephanie Evershaw-Adam and her unknown element of a husband entered the room. Stephanie's appearance pulverised any passing curiosity I may have had about him.

I'd only seen her once up to that point, and a quick drunken analysis hadn't quite prepared me for the woman who took her place at the head of the room. To her credit, she'd forgone the false and probably insincere outward signs of mourning. Her long and simple navy print dress that nipped a waist Kate Moss would diet for was finished off with a matching cotton jacket. Her dark, casually cropped hair was pushed back off her face with a broad hairband. All the better to see those startling green eyes and wide, full mouth. An advertising man's dream – those features could have sold Tory Party membership to Yorkshire miners.

I knew very little about Stephanie. She'd been far from forthcoming in our one phone call. But her address had given the game away. George had been right when he'd mentioned the art college in Manchester. I'd managed to trace her from there, though she wasn't the eternal student I'd been expecting to find. Some sort of art historian, she had enough clout to secure a post as part-time lecturer in the subject. Sita, who'd studied art herself, would get on well with her.

Stephanie was a resident of that yuppie paradise Alderley Edge, a quiet Cheshire town where a certain policeman had insinuated that anybody black from Moss Side had no right to be. Her neighbourhood was so élitist (and so paranoid) that even Julia, no stranger to the better things in life, had once been unable to gain access to the security-conscious suburb when delivering a car to a client. But for George's sake (or what lay in his will), Stephanie had decided to slum it in Calderton.

Her husband, Claude, was the male equivalent of a handbag. She'd miss him if he wasn't there, but only because she'd have nowhere to put her stuff. Admittedly I was making a bit of a snap judgement, and God forbid, that was usually Julia's territory, but so far my old friend had been unable to tear her eyes from the striking Stephanie for long enough to make any comment about the woman's spouse.

So, where did this conclusion come from? Experience, that's where. For a recently married couple, well heeled and well matched, they had very little to say to each other. Their comments, as they took their seats, were short and whispered, though, to be honest, they needed to be. Mrs Buckham, as AnnaMaria had once said, 'had ears like a shit-house rat'. I always thought that was a reference to eyes, not ears, still, it fitted either organ. Anyway, Stephanie's irritation with Claude was plain to see. A frown flickered over that lovely and line-free forehead more than once and the smile that she offered when finally she acknowledged her audience was as false as Disneyland.

'I'd like to thank you all for coming, especially under such circumstances,' she began in a deep and polished voice. Her voice was the only thing that reflected her true age. Visually, thirty maybe. Aurally, nearer forty.

'Most of you will have known George much better than I did. In truth, I'd only met him occasionally when I was a child, though my reason for visiting him this time is something I will never now be able to explain.' She paused before continuing, as though overcome by the event. For one odd moment I got the impression she expected to be challenged. 'But George was a stickler for etiquette...' (he wouldn't even have known what that meant) 'and, as the closest relative, it was his wish that I attend and present this service. I have Ms Campbell to thank for contacting me several months ago.'

She glanced around and looked for me among the small gathering of friends and family. I raised my hand to acknowledge her, somewhat embarrassed. She held my gaze for a moment and smiled. It was impossible not to smile back. Julia grazed my ribs gently with her elbow.

'My mother used to speak highly of her brother, though they'd drifted apart over the years, and before her death some time ago she made it clear that she'd like to resume their relationship. Sadly, that wasn't to be...'

What followed was the usual well-meaning flannel from an almost stranger to a person no longer in a position to pull her up. The liturgy didn't take long and we weren't much wiser after the event. Cousin Florence left then, seeming more confused than ever, and despite the sandwiches on offer (not particularly appealing in George's wreck of a kitchen) Julia and I decided to leave too. But not before Stephanie nabbed us at the front door.

'Ms Campbell and...?' She held her hand out to Julia.

'Julia Rossi.' I made the introductions.

Julia beamed.

'I'd like to thank you for coming today,' she said in those husky tones. 'And for contacting me in the first place.' She smiled that deadly smile. 'You must have been close to George,' she said.

'I suppose,' I replied awkwardly, embarrassed all over again. 'We looked out for each other. I've known him years. It was terrible to hear about his death. It must have been a shock to you,' I went on.

'Did he ever mention me, Ms Campbell?' she asked.

'Only a few months ago,' I said, surprise in my voice at the unexpected question. 'And please, it's Letty.'

She took my arm and suddenly I felt as though I was the most important person there. She guided me into the yard. Julia was left floundering at the door, and out of the corner of my eye I saw Claude pounce.

We were alone, the afternoon sunshine beating down on us. Stephanie's perfume floated around my head. I couldn't put a name to it but realised with a start that I would always recognise it again.

'Why do you ask?' I stammered, thrown by Stephanie's intimacy.

She released my arm and I forced myself to take a small step backwards. Get a grip, Campbell, I thought with a sigh.

'Partly curiosity, I suppose,' she replied, adding quietly, 'though there is some unfinished business.' Her bright smile was suddenly back, orthodontically perfect white teeth flashing behind soft and sensuous lips. 'Are you sure I can't interest you in some food?'

'No, I'm fine,' I said quickly. 'My partner will be wondering where I am,' I lied.

'Oh?' she asked, and cocked her head to one side. The light caught that fine porcelain skin. Her expression was suddenly inquisitive and I became more uncomfortable by the minute. 'Is he a farmer too?'

'She,' I corrected. 'Anne's a librarian.'

Stephanie had been in Mrs Buckham's company for more than five minutes; I couldn't believe she didn't know. But for whatever reason, her look of surprise seemed genuine. And then she held my gaze, smiling again. I felt myself blush from my boots upward. I'd start babbling if this continued.

'Perhaps we can meet for drinks this week?' she said finally and glanced away. 'Actually I do really need to see you. I want to discuss something with you, if you can spare the time. And of course if you've got stories about George, I'd love to hear them.'

43

'Okay,' I found myself saying, drawn not only to her but also to her odd request, and I rattled off my phone number. She didn't write it down. 'I've already got your number,' she said, softening the double entendre with that unforgettable smile. 'Anyway, I must see to my other guests.'

She held out her hand and I shook it slowly, only remembering to breathe again when she'd left.

'What was that all about?' Julia asked as we trailed home. 'What did she want? She's beautiful, isn't she?'

'I don't really know and, yes, she's gorgeous,' I had to admit.

'Her husband's a bit odd.'

'Oh? Mrs Buckham seemed to take to him. She reckoned he was charming.'

'Oh, he's that all right. He's got charm by the bucket-load. He's got a really unusual accent. I couldn't place it at all,' Julia offered. 'Mind you, I did feel as though I was being interrogated. I was hardly close to George, was I? Scarcely knew anything about him, even less about the farm,' she mumbled.

'She wants to meet,' I blurted, still distracted by thoughts of Stephanie.

'Looks like you've trapped, Campbell,' Julia hooted.

'All of us,' I said, distorting the truth. 'Not just me.'

Embarrassment floored me again. Diplomatically Julia looked away.

'Yeah, right,' she couldn't help but add. 'Lust is it?' she asked quietly, turning to me. A half-mocking smile played around her mouth. Sometimes Julia knew me better than I knew myself.

'No!' I snapped. 'Don't be ridiculous, and I'll tell Anne,' I added hastily, though with things already a bit tricky in that area of my life the prospect didn't appeal.

'Touchy,' Julia murmured, though she knew well enough not to pressure me any more.

It was odd, but I suddenly felt strangely guilty and I was reluctant to consider why. We walked the rest of the way home in thoughtful silence, a strange and unacknowledged sense of anticipation lurking hollowly in the pit of my stomach.

Chapter 9

By Tuesday the service, and Julia's observations, had all but been forgotten in the excitement of sending AnnaMaria and her baby off to Milan.

We'd already been visited by the police and bombarded with questions about George's last movements. And though we tried to be as helpful as possible, our drink-affected memories were never going to throw any light on the investigation. Sergeant Sam and WPC Emma had given up as we'd begun to repeat ourselves. We'd promised the usual 'if we remember anything else we'll be in touch', and they'd left, whispering together.

Julia, already ensconced as our house guest, was suddenly friends with AnnaMaria again and had offered to run her and Liam to the airport. To mark the occasion she'd 'borrowed' one of the cars from the forecourt and, as the MG Midget had already been sold, she used the next best thing. A survivor of the Sixties, the Rover 2000 had been drawing admiring glances for the last six months but no cash, and Julia had been forced to consider reauctioning it, so this trip out would probably be its last. Photos were taken to mark the event and Anne and I waved them off during the early hours of Tuesday morning.

'I'll ring when we arrive,' AnnaMaria promised from the leather rear seats of the portly grey car. '*Arrivederci, bella!*' she bellowed to us as Julia eased the classy vehicle down the road.

'She so wants to impress Julia's mum, you know. She's wasted in that garage,' Anne declared.

Anne would dearly have loved her niece to go down the university route, but hands-on work was the stuff that thrilled AnnaMaria. She'd had no desire to do a degree. 'All day with those middle-class gobshites? Do me a favour! Anyway, who wants to be that poor?' she'd said when the subject came up. But still Anne dreamed of the day. 'It was a happy time for me,' Anne had confessed. 'It got me away from my mother for one thing,' she'd added, reminding me of their difficult but rarely mentioned relationship.

When the car had completely disappeared from sight, we returned to a shadowy and eerily quiet house. A lone child-sized sock lay forlornly on the kitchen table and at the sight of it Anne promptly burst into tears.

'Ignore me,' she said, dabbing at her eyes.

I held her close and whispered sweet rubbish in her ear. After a moment she quietened. 'I'll just miss them,' she explained with a last sob.

'I know. So will I. Come on, it's still early, let's go back to bed.'

I took her hand and led her through the quiet house to our oasis of a bedroom. The only temptation within these four walls was beside me.

Chapter 10

If the remembrance service had been odd, the funeral itself, held almost a week after the release of George's body, was positively surreal.

The post-mortem hadn't actually explained much more than we already knew. A report in the *Echo*, penned once more by Janice, showed that George had in fact drowned, though a crack on his head was still unexplained. Reading between the lines, it was clear the police still weren't sure whether there'd been another person involved, nor was there proof of any kind of struggle (his house was in such a state, it would have been impossible to tell anyway), and, as Mrs Buckham had pointed out, there was no obvious theft.

The farm had been dusted for fingerprints but there'd been so many it would have taken years to eliminate everyone who had ever visited the place. Gossip and various theories flew around the village, some would have won prizes for their inventiveness. And then there were the rabbits... The police were in obvious attendance at the funeral and George's body, carried in by mates from the Frog and Bucket, awaited its final resting place, having been secured to a trolley beneath the pulpit.

The local Methodist minister was poorly and instead the district minister, or area manager, as Mrs Buckham somehow confused his title, would usher George towards eternal rest. The deceased's niece, who despite her promises hadn't been in touch, took the front pew with her husband, Claude. She caught my eye just once and waved at me. Self-conscious and uncomfortable, I signalled a greeting. The few other dim and distant relatives dotted the church. Cousin Florence was there again, seemingly more bemused than ever. George's neighbours huddled together in the last three pews, with Mrs Buckham at the head.

We had one late arrival.

Normally Julia was dismissive of religion and the most bigoted of Ulster Unionists would be hard pressed to beat her criticism of the Pope. Despite this, however, a couple of things could still get her to her knees: midnight mass at Christmas, especially with a couple of whiskies inside her, and her mother. The first for barely remembered religious reasons, the second for money. And while even she realised that genuflecting at a Methodist funeral was inappropriate, she had been unable to resist the opportunity to dress up. A mantilla of the finest-quality black silk lace was draped across her head, its sombre lines lending a bleak and tragic aura to the proceedings. Her dark frock, silk to match the headdress, somehow met with Mrs Buckham's approval and she edged along the pew to give Julia space to sit.

We were parked behind and to the right of the two women. I glanced at Anne to see if she had any whispered comment to make.

I'd mentioned, vaguely, the prospect of drinks with the Evershaw-Adams at some unspecified date in the future

49

and Ann, fortunately, had shown only a passing interest. Negotiations with her agent and publisher were hotting up and she had either no time on her hands or other things on her mind. Whatever the distractions were, they weren't shared with me. The funeral's bizarre quality had gripped her, though, and on spying Julia she'd shut her eyes and her hand was clamped across her mouth. Her chest was heaving and I thought for a moment she was crying. And she was. With laughter.

I tried not to look at her again, though the old beech pew shook with her convulsions. George wouldn't so much spin in his grave as do the light fantastic.

The heads of Julia and Mrs Buckham joined together briefly in conversation before the organist, Rona, a respectable, bespectacled woman I recognised from the local shop, struck up the opening chords of 'Abide with Me'. Normally this age-old and graceful Wembley favourite would have had me in floods of tears. Not so at George's funeral. Delivered in a style delightfully her own, Rona's zealous organ-playing defeated the congregation as they struggled to keep up. By the time we hit the chorus for the second time, we were doing a fair rendition of barber-shop singing. The organist, oblivious to the mayhem she was causing, launched into the third verse, her Hammond organ incongruously keeping time with an unforgettable Latin beat. Rona picked up pace. It was a race to the finish and the dysfunctional choir let rip. All but Anne, whose pretty face was still hidden behind her hands. She was sobbing by now.

Rona finished the hymn with a big chord, more Righteous Brothers than righteous, and the off-key baritones and stretched sopranos made a last effort to remain tuneful. It was a relief to stop. Anne managed to get herself under control just as the minister took the pulpit. Sadly, the rest of the show didn't have quite the same appeal and Rona managed to squeeze in only one more song before George's body was wheeled from the church into the graveyard beyond.

We traipsed after the body in straggly single file. Stephanie and Claude retired a short distance away and only George's ageing friends and immediate neighbours were left to witness the lowering of his body.

This should have been a much more sombre affair, and it was, until a drinking buddy, overcome by his emotions, slung a bottle of Guinness onto the lowered coffin. The glass burst with a heart-stopping crash against the cheap wood and its fizzy black contents soaked unappealingly into the grain. A bit like the Queen's new yacht, George was duly launched.

'So just the will now then to round things off?' Mrs Buckham commented to anyone who would listen.

We'd retired to her house for a post-funeral tea she'd insisted on staging. The word 'tradition' could have been invented by the shopkeeper. Following ancient guidelines, Mrs Buckham had set out a spread so thoroughly Old Yorkshire that it made the laws of kosher cooking look simple.

We could have any sandwich we liked as long as it had ham in it. Ham, ham and tomato, ham and pickles, cheese and ham, ham and onion, ham and jam if we wanted it. We had pork pies, sausage rolls, pickled eggs, bowls of crisps, chicken legs (cold), egg and bacon flan (hot), a bit of salad and trifle for pudding. Vegetarians ('Not the strict kind,' Mrs Buckham pointed out) got tuna or John West salmon. 'I only stock the best,' she said proudly. And then there were eggs, boiled till they bounced.

'Well, you'd never starve,' Anne said drily, helping herself to a bit of everything.

I battled with a couple of rubbery free-rangers.

Mrs Buckham's house was packed. The shop was closed all day in deference to George's passing. Cousin Florence was gamely staying on till the end, as were any villagers happy to indulge in a free lunch. Only the no-drinking policy would ensure an empty house before midnight. Sooner or later the rabble would retire to the Frog and Bucket – Mrs Buckham wasn't stupid.

'She's such a dear,' Mrs Buckham told me over the trifle-laden sweet trolley.

'Who is?' I mumbled through egg white glued to the roof of my mouth.

'Cousin Florence,' she explained, daintily chewing a ham and something teacake. 'Do you know, she's eighty-two. She thought George had been dead for years,' she added with a whisper.

She looked across the room and caught Florence rummaging through her sandwich. Meat was removed with a suspicious look. Jack, the long-suffering grandson, relieved her of the ham and, short of anywhere to dump it, dropped the offending slices down the back of the settee. Mrs Buckham stiffened but resisted a shriek of horror.

'Jack's not really her grandson,' she confided when she'd recovered from the shock. 'Never had children of her own. Anyway, I had a word with that gold-digger, you know,' Mrs Buckham ploughed on.

'Florence?' I asked in surprise. At eighty-two her gold-digging days were surely over.

'No, that Stephanie. Mrs Evershaw-Adam, as she likes to be known.' Her voice dripped with sarcasm.

'What about?' I asked and, defeated, I dropped the last of my overcooked food onto my plate. Edwina Currie's egg scares were still being taken literally in Calderton. Egg mayonnaise was never likely to be popular.

'The will of course.' Mrs Buckham sniffed. 'Do you know, George had a solicitor. From Manchester too.

Richardson and Smedley. Have you heard of them?'

Heard of them? Who hadn't? The lower variety of royals had used these high-class solicitors. They commanded big money; even showbiz types fought for their representation. Many a drug-possession charge resulted in a caution, or was dropped altogether, due to their expertise. Richardson and Smedley had branches throughout the country and were almost as famous as their clients.

'Yes, I've seen them on the telly,' I said.

'So you know how well off you've got to be to afford them.'

'Well, yes. But this is just a simple will, isn't it?'

'Is it?' Mrs Buckham asked quietly. 'We'll see.'

Chapter 11

'Richardson and Smedley?' Julia gawped. 'God almighty! What was George doing with them? They're the crème de la crème of solicitors. They've got more influence than Richard Branson.'

We were in the pub again. The funeral tea had stuck in my throat and only two pints of Watmoughs Bitter would wash it down. Anne had declined an invite – she had an important call to make to her agent – and only Julia, who'd nipped back to the house to change into more familiar clothes and with absolutely nothing else to do, was willing to accompany me.

A transformed Frog and Bucket was heaving under the weight of an expanded clientele. John and Hilda were hard-pressed to keep up with demand. And none was more demanding than the eighty-two-year-old Cousin Florence, who could down her drinks with the best of them. Her grandson wisely stuck to bottled shandy. A Huddersfield lad of barely nineteen years, Jack's idea of hell was to be stuck in Calderton for the night. Florence, straight-backed and thin as a blade, was supported by neither stick nor arm as she made her way to our table. Her brown C&A cardie had obviously been lurking in her wardrobe since the early Seventies and was worn long, over green-trousered non-existent hips.

'I'm Florence,' she declared emphatically, as she took a seat by my side.

Any assumptions I might have had regarding her mental state were soon shattered. Rummaging in her handbag for her cigarettes, she finally lit up and took a couple of drags on her Embassy King Size before addressing me again.

'I thought George was already dead, you know,' she said with no preamble. 'Before you contacted the family at any rate.'

'Yes, Mrs Buck – '

'He was younger than me,' she interrupted. 'But we were only distantly related. I'm surprised you could find me.' She waited for a response.

'Well, he was insistent that I find every – '

'And the will-reading? That won't be like the funeral, you know. Like weddings, they bring out the worst in folk,' she declared.

She ground out her cigarette in the glass ashtray. Big enough to cause brain damage, it was as well it was screwed to the table, though how the bar staff were supposed to clean it was anybody's guess. The landlord obviously wasn't taking any chances. I glanced at Julia, who was staring unblinkingly into the far distance. No help there.

'You'll be coming to the – '

'Goodness, yes,' Florence stated in her oddly clipped accent. 'Mrs Buckham has kindly offered to put me up for a while. Such a lovely lady. And I do like it here in Calderton. You never know, I might be able to buy a little place here myself.' She chuckled and, seeing the look on my face, added, 'Only joking. If George has left me any

55

money, well, we'd best not speak ill of the dead, had we?' she said, curiously repeating AnnaMaria's words. 'No, she's the one to watch,' and she pointed to where Julia's gaze fell.

Stephanie could be seen through the open-plan bar arguing with her husband in the taproom. She looked up at that moment and my reply to Florence froze in my throat. Somehow Stephanie sensed my interest. My stomach gave a nervous little jolt. This woman – no, this *straight* woman – was bothering me. And as much as I tried to ignore the fact, simply her presence bothered me too. Crushes were usually Julia's territory, and for the first time in a long while I was glad Anne wasn't with me. She'd have seen through it all in a moment.

Dressed in black pants and a plain white T-shirt, Stephanie looked all the more dangerously attractive than she had at the funeral. She still wore the dark headband and those green eyes looked greener still. Especially when they were locked onto mine. She whispered something into Claude's ear. He waved at her dismissively and she moved away from the bar, glancing once more at me.

'Julia,' I hissed at my old friend, 'I think Stephanie's heading this way.'

'So?' she said awkwardly.

'So I don't want to speak to her.'

'Who's making you?'

'Julia!'

'Oh, all right,' she said. 'I'll head her off at the pass.' She got up, not completely unwillingly, and made for the adjoining bar door.

'I can't say I blame you,' Cousin Florence commented.

There was an uncanny similarity between Florence and Mrs Buckham. It's not surprising they hit it off.

'What do you mean?' I asked tentatively.

'Oh, I think you know, dear,' she said, adding mysteriously, 'There's nothing new on God's green earth.'

Bewildered and rather flustered, I leaned back in my chair and fidgeted with my foam-flecked glass.

'Let me fill that for you, dear,' Florence offered, and she whipped a bulging purse from her bag. 'You look like you need one.'

She tottered to the bar before I had a chance to protest, her bunion irritating shoes sinking into the unweathered carpet.

'Well, thanks for making me look a complete fucking idiot,' Julia, who'd acquired a vulgar streak from somewhere along the path of life, hissed angrily into the back of my neck.

'What?' I demanded, thrust into the present.

She moved to face me across the newly varnished table and glared. Her towering form would have intimidated anyone else, but she was so familiar to me that I could see the pussy cat beneath the attitude.

'What?' I repeated.

'Don't "what?" me?' she said, landing heavily into a chair. If the Axminster hadn't been so luxurious, she would probably have accompanied her words with the scrape of a chair leg across the floor. Julia liked to accentuate the point wherever possible. 'I think you can cross Stephanie off your list of would-be bed partners,' she suggested.

'She was never on it,' I snapped. Then, 'Why?' I asked after a pause, curious anyway.

Florence reappeared at that point, sloshing drinks across the polished table top. The frothy alcohol made a beeline straight for Julia's expensively tailored trousers. A scene ensued. Florence produced tissues from her well-stocked bag and, avoiding Julia's defensive gestures, managed to dab the growing stain around her crotch. Embarrassed doesn't even come close to Julia's reaction as the whole pub looked on. Eventually she beat a retreat to the Ladies.

'Oh, for goodness' sake, I thought she'd never go,' Florence said, taking Julia's vacant seat.

I looked at her in amazement. Mrs Buckham, who'd had a muttered conversation with her new friend at the bar, came over to join us. Deftly, she swept the remains of the spilt beer onto the floor. The Axminster wasn't quite so virginal now.

Wrapping one thin hand around her glass of mild, Florence leaned closer to me. I got a whiff of Pond's cold cream – nostalgia in a jar – and listened to what she had to say.

Chapter 12

'The babblings of a mad woman,' Julia insisted several days later. 'You are so gullible,' she concluded loftily.

We were catching the sun's rays at the front of the porch overlooking the farm. Installed the previous summer, the porch, built of glossy pine boards, angled gently in stages from the front door to the back of the farmhouse. It ended beneath the window of the spare bedroom, now temporarily occupied by Julia. I was beginning to feel as though I lived on the set of *The Waltons*.

'It sounded reasonable at the time,' I said to my companions.

I looked over at George's farm. A deserted and desolate air surrounded the place. No more news on that front yet. I closed my eyes and drifted gently on the rocking chair. I could have been anywhere in the world, from the heat of Africa to the sun-kissed bays of California. Except for the chickens, which clucked familiarly in the midday sun. Anne had nabbed the hammock and, as far as I could tell, was fast asleep.

'She's not senile, is she?' Anne asked through dry lips, disproving my assumptions. She stirred on the hammock and it moved slightly beneath her weight.

'A bit eccentric,' I offered. 'But not demented.'

'Ha!' Julia scoffed. 'They're as crazy as each other. It's not surprising old Flo won't go back to Huddersfield, she's found a soul mate in Mrs Buckham. And I think she's waiting for a windfall, you know.'

'How so?' I asked, looking over at her.

'The will. Why else would she still be here?'

'You'll be telling me she bumped George off next.'

Julia sniffed and chose not to answer.

I sat up. 'Julia, she's eighty-two!'

'All the more reason to get rid of George,' she pointed out. 'Perhaps she felt it was now or never.'

Anne chuckled. 'I can see the headlines now: "Octogenarian in murder mystery". Julia, think about it.'

Julia sniffed again. 'Old doesn't necessarily equal innocent,' she decided.

Idly I watched white clouds skitter across the blue and perfect sky.

'I suppose it was a bit wild,' I admitted retrospectively.

'A bit wild? A bit wild?' Julia repeated loudly. 'It'll be reds under the beds again next!'

Julia settled back on her recliner. Her outburst in this heat had taken its toll.

I considered Florence's outlandish suggestion as the sun battled against my Factor 15.

'Wells,' she'd offered.

'Wells,' I'd considered thoughtfully. Wells the town? Wells Fargo? Oil Wells? Orson Welles?

'Water wells,' Mrs Buckham declared. I'd played the meaningless words around in my head.

'Wells. Where you get, you know, water from.'

'Oh,' I'd said.

'I've heard,' Mrs Buckham had pressed, claiming centre stage, 'that there's a lake under George's land and that's why that Stephanie wants to get her hands on it.'

Mrs Buckham was a strapping woman past retirement age (though still working long and gossip-laden hours in her corner shop), in odd contrast to her older, almost emaciated, beer-swilling comrade.

'And this proves what exactly?'

'Well, nothing on its own,' Mrs Buckham had got in first.

'No, nothing on its own,' Florence slipped in. 'But what else is under there?'

'I don't know,' I said with a sigh. 'What else *is* under there?'

I hadn't found out. Julia had reappeared then. Having failed to dry her trousers with the hand-drying machine, she'd insisted that we leave then and there.

'We'll talk later,' Mrs Buckham hissed at my retreating back.

'After the will-reading,' Florence managed to get the final word in. Or thought she had at least. The saloon doors cut off Mrs Buckham's closing comment. '. . . proof of the pudding. . .' was all I heard her say.

I'd not got much else out of Julia either on the way home.

'Tell me what Stephanie said.'

Julia had refused to meet my eye. 'Nothing much,' she said. 'But I don't think she's gay.'

Still under the spell of a crush, I received that remark with mixed emotions. Relief was coupled with disappointment.

'Why?'

Julia hid her usual self-confidence behind a mask of indifference. She shrugged, and then it hit me.

'She didn't want to know, did she?' I crowed.

'I don't know what you mean,' she retorted, picking up speed.

Suddenly she was scurrying in front of me, kicking up little puffs of dust as we headed home. I'd never seen her move as fast.

'It doesn't stop her being a dyke,' I'd suggested to her broad, cotton-shirted back. She'd muttered something under her breath. Two words, the last one being 'off'.

That conversation would remain a private thing between me and Julia. Not usually one to keep secrets from my partner, it seemed a case of 'least said, soonest mended'.

'Still,' I said, 'finding a lake under your garden would be no bad thing, would it?' I glanced at my sweltering chums, thinking they would agree.

'Ever heard of subsidence?' Julia muttered, determined to be the bearer of sobering news.

'Ever heard of water meters?' Anne, pursuing another avenue of thought entirely, managed quietly.

We pondered this as the sun cracked the flags across the region.

'Anyway, we would have heard,' Anne pointed out. 'There aren't many well-kept secrets in Calderton.'

She paused, reaching under her T-shirt to scratch a particularly aggravating itch. I wanted to do that for her myself. Lazily she groped for the tall beaker of iced lemonade that was melting quickly by her side. I watched her, suddenly lustful, even in this stultifying heat, as the bendy straw slipped between her lips. Eyes closed, she took a couple of small gulps. A drop escaped her mouth and it ran slowly down her cheek. I wanted to lick the sticky fluid from her skin. In fact, I wanted to pour the chilled lemonade all over her body to see what interesting patterns the ensuing goose pimples would make. Under the sun's searing rays, she'd probably only blister. Smearing her in calamine lotion would be an absorbing distraction though.

God, dream on, Campbell.

'Oh,' she said suddenly. 'I've remembered why Claude Adam sounded familiar.' She groped in her shoulder bag, handily placed at the side of her seat, and after a moment spent shuffling through papers withdrew a handful of her own prose. 'Bear with me,' she mumbled. 'Ah, here we are. It's funny how you forget what you've written,' she added thoughtfully.

'Oh, I don't know,' Julia chimed in. 'I have the same problem with cheques.'

Anne chuckled. 'It's the bit I did about the war. The Second World War, that is – there've been so many.' She ad-libbed her own words 'Mmm, Claude Adam, MBE, VC. Born 1902, educated at Eton and so on. Navy career man. Joined security services during the war...'

'My name is Bond, James Bond,' I cackled.

Julia snorted at my Connery impersonation.

'...Became marginally famous for the role he played in the Nuremberg Trials. That's why I put him in my book,' Anne added. 'Died with his wife in an unexplained boating accident in 1967. Ha-ha! Survived by only son, Claude Samuel Adam,' she said triumphantly. She rummaged around again and plucked a copy of a type of *Who's Who* from the bottomless pit that was her shoulder bag. 'According to the family entry in here,' she said, flipping pages... 'This isn't the real thing by the way,' she interrupted herself to explain. 'It's more of an historical *Who's Done What to Whom*. Anyway, Sir Claude was married twice, the second wife being Mary, George Evershaw's sister, remember, and his son was by his first wife – she died in childbirth.'

I shuffled in my chair, suddenly intrigued.

'The son was palmed off with relatives at some place the family owned in Derby. He's been estranged for years. He stepped back on the scene when his father died, probably hoping for pickings from the estate. And that's it. It doesn't say what he got, though we could probably find out. Will's are public property, after all. I think. And that's all it says.' She closed the book with a snap.

'The breeding rituals of the rich,' Julia sneered.

I looked at her tailored shorts and DKNY T-shirt and didn't even attempt a comment. Oh, AnnaMaria, what an opportunity you just missed.

'So,' Julia added, 'you think it's Stephanie's husband?'

Anne shrugged. 'It fits, I suppose. I don't know how ethically sound that is. Though they're not blood-related.'

'I wonder how George's sister came to marry Sir Claude. Even George didn't know she'd had a trip down the aisle. I wouldn't have thought they mixed in the same circles,' I mused.

'Who knows?' Anne said, and settled back in her chair.

We considered this prospect, but before anyone could comment Julia's mobile phone shattered the peace. I looked up, wondering where she could possibly keep such an object among such skimpy clothing. She produced the tiny object from a hidden pocket in her shorts, its green glow ominously lighting up her hand. If these portable devices got any smaller, she'd be able to keep one in her sock.

She grunted tiredly into the handset and then suddenly sat up. 'Hiya,' she said, smiling.

'Sita,' Anne mouthed at me. The following conversation proved her wrong.

'I'm just surprised to hear from you,' Julia said. She listened for a moment. 'Yes, we seemed to have our wires crossed a little.'

She prattled on and I settled back, losing interest. Business, by the sounds of it.

Anne dragged herself from the hammock as the house phone rang. 'I'll get it,' she said. 'Do you want lemonade?'

I smiled a 'yes'.

She disappeared into the house.

'Yes, of course,' I heard Julia say. 'She's here with me now. Hold on.' She held out the phone. 'For you,' she said.

'Who?' I asked.

Julia didn't reply, just waved the object urgently in my direction. I took it, puzzled.

'Hello, Ms Campbell, it's Stephanie Evershaw-Adam here.'

Flushed, I returned the phone to Julia.

'Well?' she asked, leaning forward on her recliner. 'What did she want?'

Anne came back then, clinking glasses. She avoided my gaze, wearing an expression I couldn't place. 'You want to watch those rays. No ozone to speak of nowadays, remember.' She went back in the house to get the sun block.

Guilt made my blushes worse. Julia cackled at my predicament. 'Tart,' she whispered.

Her comment deserved the glare I gave her.

'She wants to discuss George's will,' I said in explanation.

'Yeah, over drinks, I bet,' Julia said wickedly.

'Shut up, Julia,' I snapped.

'You've really got it bad, haven't you?' Julia remarked, suddenly serious. 'You're not having problems with Anne, are you?'

'Don't be stupid!' I shot back.

'Well, you haven't been out much lately.'

'Anne's been busy, hasn't she? With her book and everything.'

We were on sensitive ground and I felt uncomfortable with Julia's comments. Especially since I'd had more than a few similar troubled thoughts myself recently.

The previous week Anne had approached me, wanting to 'talk'.

'Talk?' I'd asked warily.

'About us, where we're going...' It had felt as though even the word should have a capital 'T'. Cowardly to the end, I'd found other, more earth-shattering duties to attend to (chickens could be amazingly demanding at times). I had a horrible premonition about where such a conversation would lead. Never mind 'talk' with a capital 'T', I dreaded it would be 'problem' with a capital 'P'. Avoidance therapy Julia would have called it.

'You know I'd never do anything untoward,' I said.

Julia laughed delightedly. 'Untoward? What *have* you been reading?' She clicked her fingers together, as though a thought had just occurred to her. She pointed at me and grinned. 'You've been watching Emma Thompson films again, haven't you?'

I giggled. She knew I hated them.

There was a long pause.

'And Anne's okay, is she?' Julia went on more seriously.

'Yes.'

'It's you then! You must be having your seven-year itch early.' She laughed, relieved and pleased with her observations. 'Stick to fancying k d,' she suggested. 'No chance of discussing wills with her.'

'Who wants to discuss the will?' Anne asked, thankfully having caught only the tail end of the conversation. She handed me a tube of Sun Buster, the latest Boots summer product.

'Stephanie,' Julia said, and added mischievously, 'Over drinks.'

'Oh? When?' Anne asked, clambering back into the hammock.

'Thursday,' I told her. 'Who was on the phone?' I asked.

'Work, for me,' she replied, lying down with a sigh.

'Anything important?' I queried, when no other

information was forthcoming.

'Nothing much,' Anne mumbled. She closed her eyes.

I took a long drink of the lemonade. In truth, my parched throat had threatened to fail me during the brief telephone conversation. It felt ridiculous. It *was* ridiculous. A crush. At my age.

'I'm sorry I've not been in touch earlier, but there's something I've been wanting to discuss,' Stephanie had said in *that* voice. I'd squeaked some inane reply. The offer of drinks had come then too. '... seven-thirty okay?'

I'd stuttered an 'I'll see' and 'I'll be in touch.' It was the best I could manage.

'But what's to discuss?' Anne asked, realistically enough. 'We won't know anything until the actual reading.'

'Pah!' Julia interrupted. 'That's not till the end of the month. Sounds like sneak previews to me.'

'Is that legal?' I asked,

'Since when has that mattered?' Julia replied drily.

'Thursday's out for me. And Friday come to that,' Anne said. 'I've a meeting with Debs. Debbie Jones, that is,' she added hurriedly. 'You know, my agent?'

I knew of the woman Anne had come to rely on and also spend much of her spare time with, but I'd never met her.

'Julia?' I asked desperately.

She grinned and shook her head, black hair flipping over that extraordinarily handsome face. 'No chance. I've got needles I need to poke in my eyes.'

Anne laughed. 'Surely she's not that bad?'

Julia didn't offer a reply.

'Well, you'll just have to go on you own,' Anne said decisively.

She rocked herself with some force on the suspended bed. I had an image of her flying off the balcony to land among the chickens in the yard beyond. The thought made me shudder.

'It would be handy to be just one step ahead in the gossip stakes,' she suggested.

'I'll see,' I said, closing the subject.

And with that comment, and in that heat, and despite everything, I fell asleep.

Chapter 13

Claude was just leaving the house as I headed up Watershedding's View the following Thursday. I waited a moment as he took off in his Porsche, going in the direction of the moors. Anne's demand for gossip and Julia's unspoken challenge had driven me there. That and an itching desire to meet the woman again.

The rented house was a subdued four-bedroom detached bungalow built in the Eighties. Using locally quarried stone as decoration, these bungalows were designed to be in keeping with the rest of the area and so there hadn't been much objection to the cluster of Barratt-type properties that had sprung up at the brow of the hill. Commanding spectacular views but less spectacular prices, the small estate was home to Halifax-based doctors and other professionals. Stephanie's rented house was currently in between owners.

I parked outside the bungalow, my ageing Land Rover thundering bronchially in the muggy summer evening. The night air was still and hot; not a breath of wind rattled the well-maintained trees, though heavy storm clouds lurked overhead. Perhaps we'd have some rain at last.

I'd managed to get myself in a state about the meeting. Trying to keep my ridiculous overreaction from Anne had been a problem, especially after I'd finally decided to accept Stephanie's invitation. It didn't occur to me that we could have arranged to meet elsewhere. God, who was I kidding?

'My partner can't make it,' I'd said over the phone.

'Oh,' Stephanie had said in surprise, not having invited Anne anyway. After a moment she chuckled. 'Neither can my husband.'

She breezed on. 'I think we should get properly acquainted, don't you? We may well be neighbours, after all.'

'Yes, meeting as neighbours is a good idea,' I said senselessly, and then suddenly added an unplanned thought, 'Can I invite a friend?'

Stephanie paused. 'Yes, of course,' she said finally.

'Great, seven-thirty then. Bye.' I slammed the phone down.

Mrs Buckham didn't know it then, but she was about to become my chaperone.

Sylvia had accepted my offer quicker than an invitation to the Queen's Garden Party. Flo, her new friend and Stephanie's most distant of distant relatives, had been pissed off at her exclusion.

I shouldn't have worried about Sylvia's time-keeping. I could hear her voice drifting through the breeze blocks and stone cladding halfway down the drive. Her bike, the latest aluminium twenty-four gear lightweight mountain bike, had been abandoned among the privets. Mrs Buckham, having taken up this new hobby, had rejected next year's London Marathon, a fantasy she'd been living with for years: 'A bit old hat now. I've always liked two wheels,' she'd confessed. Mrs Buckham was grappling with the arrival of old age, and so far she was throttling the life out of it.

I rattled on the Ronsealed door and I could hear the race down the hall to answer it. The thought filled me with delight.

'Ms Campbell, please come in,' Stephanie, a breathless step ahead of Mrs Buckham, offered graciously. The unlit hallway threw Stephanie's face into silhouette.

'It's Letty,' I reminded her as I tried to pick out her features among the shadows.

A glimmer of those white teeth emphasised her languid smile.

'Your friend arrived early.'

'Oh?'

'An hour early,' Stephanie whispered with a smile, hinting at a dry wit. 'Please, come through into the sitting room.'

I followed her slim form, reminded once again of Demi Moore. Perhaps they went to the same hairdresser. Money obviously wasn't an issue in Stephanie's life, making me question suddenly why she should have any interest in her uncle's run-down farm.

I took the seat offered, my nerves less rattled than I thought they would be. Mrs Buckham dispatched herself into the kitchen to prepare drinks – 'I like to make myself useful,' she said – and I was left alone with my soon-to-be neighbour.

'I'm sorry if I sounded mysterious,' she began. 'That wasn't my intention.' She eased, cat-like, into the high-backed leather armchair opposite. Her carefully ironed jeans were cinched tightly around her waist, accentuating her dainty frame, and as she crossed her legs the dark blue material rode up around her shins. A chain of filigreed gold delicately adorned one ankle. I tried not to stare at the pale, smooth skin. She was covered in the stuff, I thought stupidly. Her sleeveless, navel-revealing

71

vest fitted loose and low over small but rounded breasts. Her vest was not like any I've ever had, from Ladybird undies worn as a child ('Keep it on, you'll catch your death,' was Mum's persistent warning) to ill-fitting green numbers I was bullied into wearing for school sports. My experience with these garments had never had sexual overtones.

Stop staring, I thought, when I realised I was. Just stop it. Now.

At some point I managed to reach her face. I gazed at those startling green eyes and noticed that her returned stare was as frank as my own.

'You wanted to discuss something?' My hurried comment was sharper than I'd intended.

'Have we set off on the wrong foot?' she enquired. A smile pulled at that wide mouth.

Discomfort made me flush slightly. 'Sorry, no,' I stammered. 'I just wondered what you know that I don't.'

'I like that,' she said. 'Not beating about the bush.'

Mrs Buckham, having produced the fastest tea since tea-bags were invented, hurried back into the sitting room. She wasn't prepared to sacrifice one moment of this.

'Sorry I took so long,' she said, easing her widening girth onto the settee next to me. 'What have I missed?'

Stephanie chuckled and reached for those special cigars from the coffee table. Funny, I wouldn't have put her down as a smoker.

'Sugar?' Mrs Buckham asked as she poured three cups of the finest Yorkshire brew.

Stephanie lit up, spirals of rich Cuban smoke drifting towards the ceiling, and shook her head.

'Eeh, look at you,' Mrs Buckham said to our hostess. 'You should have two spoonfuls at least. I've seen more fat on a greasy chip.'

Stephanie laughed aloud this time, a strong, clear,

singsong sound, something you wouldn't guess at from that slim frame. She moved slightly in her chair and more of her flat, muscular stomach was revealed. A silver stud glinted suddenly. Her belly button was pierced. The woman was forty, looked thirty and dressed like a twenty-year-old. I felt like blob of the week next to her. Even so, I was fully eroticised (despite Sylvia Buckham's presence) and I swallowed. Hard.

'Come on then,' Sylvia said, handing out tea. Not being party to the heady atmosphere, she was oblivious to the subplots going on around her. 'What's this all about?' Stephanie laid her cigar in the ashtray and got up. Despite the nipped waist, the jeans slid to her hips and the vest headed north. I put my cup back on the table. Any more of this and I'd throw it all over myself. And probably run out of the house screaming.

She went to a dark and brooding oak dresser. The house had been let fully furnished and the dresser, with its supposedly heavy, masculine style, was in keeping with the rest of the household effects. Stephanie stood with her back to us as she rummaged in a soft leather bag. Her jeans hugged firm and pert buttocks and, as she arched forward her backbone stood out clearly against that oh-so-white skin. A red and angry scar ran diagonally across her back to disappear somewhere beneath the waistband of her denims.

'Ooh, that's a nasty scar,' Mrs Buckham remarked, happy to state the obvious.

'A riding accident,' Stephanie said, explaining the injury away.

'Horses?' I ventured huskily.

'Motorbikes, professionally, years ago.' She dismissed the subject.

Somehow I couldn't imagine her astride a Honda 750. And then, suddenly, I got a clear image of that very same thing.

73

She turned to me. 'I've always been interested in racing. And I did quite well for a while.'

Heart beating thickly in my chest, I struggled for sanity and a picture of Anne. I managed to conjure up neither.

From her bag Stephanie produced a handful of envelopes that were stuffed to ripping point with letters. Clearing a space on the coffee table, she scattered them haphazardly across the oak surface. Mrs Buckham, finding it hard to believe that she was to witness Stephanie's revelations first hand, sat poised at the end of the sofa, silent in case we remembered she was there. The letters, painstakingly written in longhand, were removed from their wrappings and Stephanie fanned them across the table, like a card sharp about to do a trick.

'At the remembrance service,' she began, hands hovering over the papers, 'I said I'd called to see George.' She smiled a sad, wry smile. 'I think the fates were against us both that day.'

Mrs Buckham suddenly fidgeted, probably remembering her own misgivings about George's niece.

Stephanie went on. 'I know there has been talk in the village,' she said, as though she'd read a few minds, 'and my timing left something to be desired.'

She paused and offered me a soft wide-mouthed and lilting smile. Her talk of desire had a predictable effect on me.

She looked down at the letters, serious again. 'People would have you believe I'm mercenary,' she said bluntly. 'But apart from my uncle's estate, I really do have good reason to be here.'

Mrs Buckham, attempting to justify herself, leapt in with both feet. 'Well, it's just poor old George's interests we've got at heart, you know. We were all very fond of him.' Her cheeks shone with high spots of colour. How her nose didn't grow with the lie was a mystery to me.

Stephanie didn't answer. In fact, she looked as though she'd not heard the old woman speak at all. I almost couldn't respond to her next question.

'Letty, how well did you know your Aunt Cynthia?'

Even Mrs Buckham stopped fidgeting. The only sound was the faint and steady ticking of the hallway clock.

'I, er..., I don't know,' I stammered. 'I'm not sure I know what you mean.'

I remembered her as a rather odd woman, a private woman who, for some reason, had left me her farm. Still it came as a shock to realise that I knew hardly anything about her. As a youngster I was not used to questioning such things, so her past was a mystery to me. As I grew up we'd visit her sometimes. In those days it was what you did. As common and as predictable an occurrence as Sunday dinner.

'Why?' I asked

For reasons I couldn't fathom, I was suddenly uncomfortable with this. I wanted to snatch my question out of the air, pour my tea back into the pot and retreat to the safety of my farm. Instead I asked 'Why?' again.

'Do you know how old she was when she died?' She answered my question with another unsettling one of her own. Her eyes, a startling colour anyway, had somehow gone a shade darker.

'She was the oldest girl in the family. At least twenty years older than Mum. Why?'

That question again. Would she ever answer it?

For the first time Stephanie wouldn't look me in the face and merely fiddled with one of the letters in front of her.

'Would you mind if I read this to you?' she asked.

'Ooh no, you go ahead, love,' Mrs Buckham encouraged, folding her arms across her belly in expectation. Her breasts, already straining against a bra one step away from the bin, settled gratefully against her forearms.

'I think we're going to need something stronger than tea for this,' Stephanie suggested quietly. 'Mrs Buckham, if you wouldn't mind, there's wine in the kitchen. Pick whichever takes your fancy.'

Releasing her breasts from their resting place, she nimbly got to her feet. 'Righto love, won't be a tick.'

'May I join you?' Stephanie asked as Mrs Buckham left the room in search of alcohol.

Not trusting myself to speak, I shrugged a 'whatever'. She took the vacated seat next to me. I didn't know how to respond to that cool and lingering look; I was even less sure when she took my hand in hers.

The hallway clock hammered in my ears.

Her touch was dry and warm, and I found I couldn't reclaim my hand. I stared at my lap, where her short, blunt fingers rested against mine. I'd had guilty fantasies and lust-racked dreams about this moment, but now that it was reality...

I opened my mouth to speak. I had no idea what was going to come out.

'Stephanie, I can't...'

Her softly hissed 'shh' silenced me. Turning my left hand over, palm side up, she ran a neatly clipped fingernail sharply across my skin.

Despite my protestations, I wanted to kiss this stranger. Hell, I wanted to do a lot more than that.

She traced the markings on my palm. 'My God,' she said quietly. 'She was right.'

Chapter 14

Stepping into this other dimension had banished, at least for the moment, any lustful thoughts. Somehow it was easy, then, to reclaim my hand. My palm itched where she'd touched it.

That slow, sensuous smile that had so bewitched me was gone and a look of shock transformed her face. 'I'm sorry,' she stammered. Suddenly she looked older and unsure of herself. That confident manner had escaped her.

I looked at my hand with its mysterious lines and life-affecting creases which seemed no different from before. I rubbed it against my jeans to stop the deep-seated itch.

Suddenly there was a loud bang from the kitchen that made us both jump.

Mrs Buckham giggled and burst through the door clutching a bottle of foaming Bollinger and three lager glasses. When Stephanie had asked her to get a bottle of wine I don't think vintage champagne was quite what she had in mind.

'This looked nice,' she said. 'I think some of it went on the floor.'

Yeah, twenty quid's worth, by the looks of it.

I turned to Stephanie. It was obvious wasted champagne wasn't her immediate concern. She reached for my hand again and, though the itch was gone, a clear and definable red mark was beginning to appear, the edges of skin swelling slightly where her nail had traced a pattern. Perhaps I was allergic to Stephanie. It was the best reason I'd come up with so far for not seducing her.

'Have you been eating strawberries?' Mrs Buckham asked, peering at my upturned hand as she squeezed herself back on the settee.

Stephanie retreated to her chair.

'My husband used to react like that. It's a wonder it didn't kill him. Strawberries turn up in all sorts of things,' she added innocently. It suddenly became uncomfortably clear why Mrs Buckham's shop had always been well stocked with a particular fruit jam. Maybe it was lucky for her that her husband hadn't been subjected to a coroner's report himself.

'I'm sorry,' Stephanie repeated, looking slightly sheepish.

Mrs Buckham poured champagne, stopping to check every now and again that we'd all got the same amount.

I was ready for a drink. My mouth felt like I'd been chewing emery boards.

'I found these letters when I was clearing out George's loft. They're copies and I've no idea why George should have had them. From what I can make out, they don't seem to have anything to do with him.' She paused to take a swig of the Bollinger. 'Look, I'll read this one,' she suggested, as pale as milk. 'It's the letter with the latest date. Maybe things will be a little clearer then.'

Stephanie read the date: 25th March 1948. Postmark,

San Francisco, USA. 'Dear C,' she began, her voice trembling slightly.

> It's still not possible to come to you, much as I would like. For almost five years we've kept our secret. I really hope that only the three of us know of it now. I see your brother almost every day. His trip to the docks takes him past my little shop, but we only speak when I have a letter for you. He looks haggard, worn down by it all. I read of his dealings during the early days of the Nuremberg trials. What a terrible time that must have been for him. To be witness, even to the aftermath of such atrocities, must have been such a burden. And for him to carry secrets of his own must be awful too. But it is not time, it may never be the right time, to reveal what we know. I'm so sorry for the tone of this letter. I, like you, want to write of happier times, of our summers together in England before I had to leave. And one day I will, but for now I must know that our acquisitions are safe.

Stephanie paused to take a drink of wine. I looked at Mrs Buckham. She was goggle-eyed and open-mouthed at what she was hearing. I suppose my own reaction was mirrored in her face. Stephanie went on:

> Reassure me, reassure your brother when you write to him, I know he worries constantly too. I don't need to tell you how careful you must be. Who knows if our correspondence, much less anything else, is safe from prying eyes. Your brother does his best and he insists that diplomatic immunity protects him, but he is more trusting than I am.
>
> When those responsible for the evil of the last few years are behind bars, then maybe we can return what we possess to the rightful owners. But not yet. Europe, as you know, is still in chaos and too corrupt to hand

over that which you have hidden so well.

Stephanie paused again, clearly overcome by the letter. Mrs Buckham took a deep breath, ready to launch into who, why and what until I nudged her into silence.

I have one piece of news for you. I am to return home to Prague. My mother is very ill and I feel I must go. I never thought I would see Europe again, and with my homeland in such turmoil part of me wants to stay here in America; it is a safe place for me. But I will go to Prague. My mother expects it and I so want to see her again.

I will write to you on my return.

My love to you, Imrie.

Chapter 15

There was a long expectant silence. Even Mrs Buckham held back. Stephanie slumped in her seat, her pale skin almost translucent now.

'Do you know what it means? What acquisitions were they on about,' I asked after a moment.

'I'm not sure. Perhaps with your help, Letty, I can find out, and you too, Mrs Buckham.'

'Ooh, if I can,' the older woman said excitedly.

'It's probably best that as few people as possible know about this, though if you hear of any local folklore or rumours, Mrs Buckham, perhaps you could let me know? I also think Anne should be kept out of it. What do you think?' There was a significant pause as Stephanie looked carefully at me.

'Any particular reason?' I asked.

'No, not really. Just a thought.' She kept eye contact for a moment. I suppose it seemed a reasonable request under the circumstances.

'Of course,' I said. 'If that's what you want.' I didn't realise then just how easy it would be to keep my word.

'And Florence too, if that's all right.'

Mrs Buckham was crestfallen. She would have broken the world land-speed record on her mountain bike to spread the news given half a chance.

I don't know how Stephanie expected her to keep anything confidential. Mrs Buckham had as much respect for secrets as the lions had had for Christians.

'On my husband's grave,' she promised. 'And on my own life,' she added hastily, seeing my doubtful expression.

Stephanie slowly gathered together the letters, carefully replacing them in their various envelopes.

'Who is "C"?' I asked as Stephanie stacked letters.

'You don't know?' She paused, her eyes roving across my face looking for what? A lie, I guessed from her odd expression.

'You don't, do you?'

'Should I?' I asked the beautiful woman before me. I suddenly realised we were playing the same strange mental game that AnnaMaria and Julia were so good at.

'I'm sorry, I thought I'd made it clear.'

Stephanie began to fiddle with her wedding ring. Not some plain gold thing either. Embedded with jewels designed to catch the light and its unusual markings were Egyptian-influenced, and not an Egyptian influence of the Nineties by the looks of it. This had a Twenties nostalgic feel from a time when any explorer worth his salt was digging up tombs and the accompanying treasure. Her ring was the only thing that actually shrieked of money. Stephanie was definitely a low-key kind of gal.

'That's a lovely ring,' Mrs Buckham said, gazing at the piece of jewellery. 'Where did you get it?' She knocked back her champagne.

'Thank you,' Stephanie replied, sliding the ring around her finger. 'A gift. From my stepfather.'

Mrs Buckham waited for further information and,

when no more surfaced, I was forced to intervene.

'You were saying,' I prompted.

'From what I can gather, "C" is, or was, your Aunt Cynthia.'

I swallowed to relieve my mouth of its sudden dryness. 'And Imrie?'

'Her lover. Her female lover.'

Mrs Buckham, as much a fan of melodrama as the next person, squeaked, 'Cynthia?' then looked at me accusingly, as though my genes or hormones or whatever were to blame.

'She never said anything to me,' she grumbled, hating the idea of having missed out on such rich gossip.

'Judging by the letters, she didn't say anything to anybody,' Stephanie assured her.

There was a moment's stony silence, broken only by the shuffling of papers and the intimidating sound of the hallway clock.

'Do we get to see the rest of these then?' I asked.

Stephanie fixed her eyes on me and lust, even at this inappropriate moment, grabbed me by the throat.

'You can take these copies, though there is one small problem,' she said. 'Not all of them are in English. And some of them are a combination of several languages. Czech, what looks like Dutch, and several in Italian. A real mixed bag.' She smiled. 'How are your language skills?'

I smiled back. 'Non-existent. If you can't make a lot of sense of them, why do you think I'll do better?' I asked.

'Perhaps you won't,' she said simply. She left her chair to fumble in her bag and once more the vivid scar across her back was exposed. I had a sudden fantasy of raking my tongue across it. A disturbing and vaguely unhealthy thought.

I reached to Mrs Buckham for reassurance. She patted my hand in response.

'I wonder if your mother knows,' she asked idly.

'I suppose. She's very close to her brother,' I managed.

Stephanie sat opposite me again and handed me a clutch of letters. She leaned forward, her top revealing more of her breasts than I could happily deal with at this moment.

'Did Cynthia ever talk about the war?'

I leaned as far back in my seat as I could manage, her cleavage retreating to a more comfortable, shadowy black 'V'.

She wasn't old enough,' Mrs Buckham interrupted, not giving a damn whether Stephanie showed her body off or not. I doubted if she'd notice if our host had been naked.

'I think you'll find that she was,' Stephanie replied.

Suddenly my hand began to itch again. I was reluctant to investigate the cause.

'And what was this all about?' I asked as I tried to relieve the strange prickly sensation.

'Let me see,' Stephanie demanded quietly, and, reaching for my hand, she opened my palm to look.

'The explanation, at least for this, isn't quite as bizarre as you might think,' Stephanie said, her finger following the same pattern across my hand that she'd made earlier. 'The letters revealed quite a bit about your aunt.'

She paused before plunging ahead. Mrs Buckham, leaning over my shoulder, breathed noisily into my ear. I got a faint waft of 4711 cologne, its citrus-based simplicity contrasting with Stephanie's thirty-five quid an ounce French fragrance.

'Imrie, the author of these letters, was, as far as I can gather, Czech by birth.' Stephanie clucked her tongue, carefully choosing her words. 'I didn't really want to get into this.'

'What do you mean?' Mrs Buckham asked.

'Imrie, somehow, recognised in Cynthia some talent,

some...oh, what's the word?'

'Gift?' Mrs Buckham offered.

Stephanie smiled. 'Yes, gift. I'm a bit cynical of such things, but Imrie believed your aunt had an ability.' She paused again. 'For second sight I suppose. Enough belief anyway to make a small drawing of some marks she found on Cynthia's hand. The marks on your hand, Letty, are almost identical.'

Mrs Buckham, happy to believe anything as long as it was outlandish enough, gasped. Stephanie, however, looked embarrassed by these revelations. I suspected her truths were usually found within the pages of the *Financial Times*.

'And you're saying that I've...' I couldn't bring myself to finish the sentence.

A slight flush crept to Stephanie's pale cheeks. 'The mark is clearly very similar,' she said, emphasising her point. 'You'll see for yourself when you read the rest of the letters.'

Her gaze settled on me as Mrs Buckham wrestled my hand open. It was a fair bet that come morning, half my neighbours would be lined up outside the farm, ready to cross my palm with silver.

'Your mother never said anything, I take it?'

'My mother wouldn't believe anything like that even if she dreamed up the winning lottery numbers.'

Stephanie laughed, a sound of relief. 'It's probably not important,' she said.

Important enough for correspondence to go backwards and forwards across the Atlantic, but I didn't comment. One more curious incident in a night of curious incidents.

Stephanie continued, 'I think you'll find other references in the letters of equal interest. Maybe you could let me know what you think of the stuff you understand. There's a connection there somewhere and they say two heads are better than one.' She smiled at me and got up. 'I'm sorry to rush you,' she said, embarrassed to dismiss us but checking her watch. 'It's just that my husband will be home soon. He doesn't really approve of all this.'

Suddenly Stephanie seemed much younger than her years. Almost vulnerable. Almost afraid. She headed for the door and I quickly got to my feet. I can take a hint with the best of them.

'It seems that George had been hoarding these letters for decades, presumably at Cynthia's request. He had so much junk I nearly missed them. We, George and I that is, had kept in touch by letter after you'd tracked me down. You didn't know?' she asked, registering my blank look.

I shook my head.

'He wanted to get in touch with me again.' She paused for a thoughtful moment. 'Though it's a shame we never quite got it together to actually meet. A fifty-year-old mystery which is likely to stay that way.'

'Don't count on it,' Mrs Buckham declared, finishing her champagne and giving the bottle a final check to make sure it was empty. 'Our Letty's very resourceful, aren't you, love?'

I smiled, only half-aware of Mrs Buckham's words, and wondered why George hadn't told me more about Stephanie, and why he'd never shown me Cynthia's letters.

'Perhaps you could speak to your mother. Assuming they were close?' Stephanie's voice lifted gently, her sentence turned into a question that I couldn't answer. She tucked her arm into mine, a disturbingly intimate gesture whether intended or not. I left it where it was.

And speak to my mother? She'd think I'd flipped – one plank short of a scaffold. Mysteries, however old and however connected to the family they might be, did not move her. She loved Sara Paretsky's *VI Warshawski* detective novels, but would always read the last chapter first so as to avoid any nasty surprises. Still, I would have a word with her, even if it meant I had to follow her to Skegness to do so. I was sure she would have something to say about all this, though it might just be 'mind your own business'.

'Right,' Mrs Buckham interrupted. 'I'm off.' She pulled on a hideous foam helmet and headed for the door. Sylvia the cycling mushroom. Despite her promises, I suspected she would have chewed Florence's ear off by morning.

I slipped the copies of Cynthia's letters into the cavernous pockets of my pants. Mrs Buckham waved goodbye to Stephanie and barely brushed my cheek with her lips before she was dashing down the hallway, out of the front door and astride her bike, her generous rump disappearing from sight as she headed down Watershedding's View.

I was left alone with Stephanie at the doorstep.

'She'll let it slip, won't she? Stephanie asked with a grin.

'Probably,' I said. 'But only to Florence. They'll have conjured up all sorts by tomorrow. Did you know her? You know, before the funeral.'

Stephanie looked thoughtful. 'I didn't know he had a cousin Florence to be honest. He certainly never mentioned her. Why?'

'Just curious. She seemed to think George had been dead for years.'

'Oh, well.' She shrugged and turned to me. 'I'm so pleased to have met you properly at last, despite the strange circumstances.'

I smiled, uncomfortable and breathless all at the same time.

'Perhaps we could meet again?' she suggested, and added hurriedly, 'If only to discuss the letters.'

'Yes,' I said. 'I'd like that. I'd like that very much.'

It was only when it was too late that I realised how much of myself I'd given away. My discomfort got worse and then I found myself hugging her goodbye. For one moment, for a fraction of a second too long, I felt her tight muscular body crushed against my own and tantalisingly, perhaps accidentally, her hand clutched the small of my back. There was enough sexual tension in the air to burn the house down. Sensibly, but reluctantly, I pulled away.

'I'll call you,' she said, and she kissed my cheek.

Seconds later I found myself staring at the solid wood of the front door.

God, who did I have to take to chaperone me next time? The whole of the *Gladiators* team?

I made my way back to the Land Rover, reluctant to rely on my slightly unsteady legs. Giving myself a moment to recover, I tapped my pockets to check I'd still got the letters, stuck the key in the ignition and slowly set off home, guilt, once more, clinging furtively to my shoulder.

Chapter 16

By the time I'd got back from my extraordinary meeting with Stephanie, I'd managed to regain some of my composure. Driving towards the farm, I saw lights burning throughout the house. Not Anne's doing; she was out shmoozing with her agent. It was far more likely to be Julia. To her, switching lights off was an unknown concept.

But it wasn't either of the two women.

AnnaMaria lay sprawled across the settee. In sleep, her bottom jaw rested almost on her chest. She could have caught a whole squadron of flies. There was no sign of toys, though, and no hint of Liam. I stroked her forehead with a forefinger. Her jaw snapped shut and her eyes flew open in panicky confusion.

She grinned, finally, in recognition. 'Letty, how're tricks?'

'Fine,' I said, returning her smile. 'But what, O tired one, are you doing here? And where's the lad?'

'Welcome home to you too!' she said, laughter in her eyes. She eased herself to a sitting position and clutched her forehead. 'Ow!' she complained. 'That fucking journey was a nightmare. Delayed at that end, delayed at this. I thought I'd never get home.'

'And you're home because?'

'Make me a cuppa and I'll explain. I want Yorkshire tea, two sugars, and a fried egg butty. On white bread. And an aspirin,' she demanded.

She got up, kissed me on the forehead and hugged me hello. Contrary to her aunt, she'd put on a couple of pounds. Olive oil and temperatures in the eighties had filled and tanned that pretty face. She looked wonderful: healthy, happy and relaxed. It was just odd to see her without her son.

'Liam's fine,' she confirmed. 'Julia's mum has taken him to the coast for the week. Milan was absolutely boiling. He was having almost as good a time as me; he probably won't even notice I've gone.'

There was a sudden but brief wistful look on her face. 'But I couldn't miss Anne's birthday, could I?'

I grinned. My planned special dinner for two would be a family affair after all.

'Where is she anyway?' AnnaMaria asked.

'Out planning strategies with her agent. It's all secret handshakes and mystery rendezvous when publishing dates get near.'

'Yeah, I noticed the manuscript was gone.'

'I didn't realise it was completely finished,' I said, hurt that Anne hadn't told me.

'Have you met her yet?' AnnaMaria asked as she washed her hands at the sink.

'Who?'

'The agent.'

'No,' I said. 'I've spoken to her on the phone once or twice. She's ever so, ever so,' I said, alluding to her Oxbridge accent. 'Pleasant enough, though. Anne reckons she's great. I suppose she is. She's got her plenty of work.'

AnnaMaria sniffed. A 15 per cent cut was about 14 per cent too much as far as she was concerned.

I suddenly squeezed AnnaMaria's coltish body. I didn't realise just how much I'd missed her.

'How long are you stopping?' I asked.

'Just the week, while Liam's at the seaside. And then another week in Italy. I can't live on fresh air after all. How is the garage?' she asked after a moment. 'And Julia,' she added with a grin.

'Ticking over, by all accounts. She was pig sick about the fashion show. How did it go?'

AnnaMaria's grin broadened. 'It got to her then?'

'I'll say!'

We'd received a postcard from AnnaMaria just days after her departure.

Dear All,
Weather fab, the days are hot and the nights are warm enough for shorts.

Julia, reading the card aloud, had pursed her lips, remembering her arguments with AnnaMaria over clothes.

Sophia has made us both wonderfully welcome. She is so generous, I'm amazed it doesn't run in the family.

Julia had gone a strange shade of purple at that.

Anyway, must dash. We've got a shopping trip organised and Sophia is taking me to see Galliano's new autumn collection and I don't want to be late. One thing, Letty. Make sure Julia is up to date at the garage. I don't want to come home to a load of paperwork. And don't let her dump it on Andy either.

See you soon.
Much love, AnnaMaria and Liam.

'I made it up, you know.'

'What?'

'The fashion show. Imagine me there? I can't think of anything worse. Julia might be a designer victim but I'd be happier at a car boot sale.'

I despaired of them both. They'd still be playing this game well into doddery old age.

'You know she's still here?' I asked. She nodded, grinning. 'Have you got to a darts match yet?'

I rummaged in the fridge for eggs, butter and a slowly defrosting loaf.

'Darts? Christ, no. We've still got this palaver with George and his will. And we haven't heard anything else about his death either.'

I suddenly remembered the minefield that was Stephanie and her odd letters. I tried to concentrate on the egg sandwich.

'I'll come with you to the reading, if I'm back in time,' AnnaMaria offered. 'Hey, he might have left you something.'

'Only a headache so far,' I laughed. 'And a bit of a mystery too.'

'Oh?' AnnaMaria said. 'Give.'

I shuffled a bubbling egg around the frying pan as I debated revealing all. I made a decision. 'Not a word to anyone, promise?'

'Cross my heart, blah de blah,' she said excitedly.

'Well, it's something to do with my aunt who owned this place?'

'Go on,' she urged.

I began to recount my tale.

She'd eaten her egg sandwich and was on to her second cup of tea by the time I'd finished.

'So what is this big secret then? And what are these – what did she call them – acquisitions?' she asked finally.

'Well, that's the thing, isn't it? Who knows? What is this link between George and my aunt? What is it exactly that she was supposed to hide for her friend, her girlfriend or whatever she was? Not to mention all this gypsy stuff,' I said examining my hand.

AnnaMaria frowned. 'Have you had a look at the letters yet?'

'I've not had a chance.'

'No time like the present,' she reasoned.

I glanced at the clock above the sink. 'It's two o'clock,' I said in surprise. 'Tomorrow is soon enough. Those letters have been knocking about for fifty years. Another day isn't going to make much difference.'

'Yeah,' AnnaMaria agreed. 'I'm shattered. Time for bed.' She said this through the type of open-mouthed yawn that dentists dream about. 'Is she home?' she asked, referring to Julia.

'Out for the night.'

'Sita?'

'No. She's still in London trying to impress Tony and Cherie. Julia's out with the darts players, though I can't imagine what the fascination is.'

'They'll be reminiscing. Three dykes at an all-girls college? I bet they've got plenty to talk about.'

'Dykes? Are they?'

'Want to put money on it?' she asked with a smirk. A brief affair with a woman when she was a teenager had left her unerringly perceptive. That and living with me. 'Anyway, Anne's a bit late, isn't she?'

She was, but I hadn't got to the worrying stage yet. When her first book hit the shops she'd been in an alcoholic daze for a week. Wined and dined by publishers, agents and eventually even the press, Anne had wandered about with a big grin on her face, enjoying all the attention.

'It's these champagne socialists,' I remarked. 'They never know when to call it a day.'

'Or night,' AnnaMaria observed. 'We'll talk in the morning then.' She kissed me on the cheek. 'Night,

Letty,' she said and stumbled off to bed.

I waited on Anne for another twenty minutes but I'd had a bit of a day of it myself and so I fell, alone and exhausted, into bed.

I didn't know it then, but despite all the strange goings-on this was the last truly happy night I was to spend for quite some time.

Chapter 17

Waking up to find Anne by my side would have been a relief, but her half of the mattress was cold and bare. I checked the bedside clock. Four-thirty. Where the hell was she? I fought off that 'oh-my-God-she's-lying-in-a-ditch-dead-somewhere' feeling and instead struggled into my dressing gown. I stood for a moment trying to breathe some life into my sleep-befuddled brain. Sounds of voices drifted up the stairs, murmurings and soft familiar laughter echoing in the stillness of the early morning.

Relief was replaced by a twinge of anger. You know the feeling. Once when I was about eight my mother insisted I accompany her on a shopping trip. Bored and then distracted by a Doctor Who display, I'd wandered into Woolworths. My mother found me, with the help of a policeman. She was so pleased to see me whole and healthy, she issued a quick lesson in parental concern. She walloped me. I never wandered off again.

Not that that was my intention with Anne. Please! Our verbal assaults were as rare as lesbians at No. 10.

I followed the sounds of laughter, clutching my

threadbare dressing gown around me (I assumed she had guests and I didn't want to frighten them to death).

'Hello,' I warned as I headed for the kitchen.

'Letty?' Anne said in surprise. 'I thought you were asleep.'

'I was just a bit worried,' I said, and popped my head around the kitchen door.

Only a small lamp illuminated the room.

'Letty,' Anne said, swirling wine around her glass. 'You've not met Debbie, have you? Debbie, Letty. Letty, Debbie.'

I moved into the kitchen, only too aware of my appearance. Debbie Jones was perhaps my age, maybe a little less. A round cherubic face smiled a greeting and I leaned over to shake hands. Her grip was firm and testing, as were those too wise eyes. Her hair, auburn and parted to one side, was cut straight to fall slightly over one eye. She ran her fingers through it to get a clearer picture of me. She was be-suited à la Rhona Cameron, rather butch, and I suddenly felt uneasy.

'I hope I haven't disturbed you,' she said, settling back into her seat. The voice was an octave lower when not distorted by phone lines. Those rich St Catherine's College tones set her up there with Julia's crowd. She was so far removed from me that only a radical makeover (my death and rebirth as a royal, for example) would close the gap between us.

'Not at all,' I lied. 'I have to get up early to see to the hens.' Yeah, but not this early, I thought testily. 'Are you staying over?' I asked, feeling as gauche as a fifteen-year-old.

'Oh no,' she said smiling. 'Don't worry, I'll head off. I think Anne and I have discussed all we need to.'

She gave Anne a big, sickening grin. I wasn't worried – threatened maybe, but not worried. I suddenly had an urge to knock her teeth out.

'I'll go and shower,' I said, mostly to Anne but for Debbie's sake as well, just in case she thought I always looked like this. 'It's been nice meeting you.' More lies.

'Sure,' Debbie said, offering her hand once more. 'I look forward to seeing you again.'

Now who's lying?

I headed back upstairs, aggravated. I'd made hasty judgements before, but this time I'd been caught on the hop, disadvantaged by circumstances. Anyway, I was tired.

I walked past the bathroom, not in the least tempted by warm water, and climbed back into bed. Despite a desperate need for sleep, I tossed and turned for half an hour. I fell asleep alone.

Two hours later I woke up that way too.

Chapter 18

The hens drove me crazy that morning. They were out of the chicken coop faster than greyhounds out of the traps at Belle Vue. To watch them eat, you'd think there'd been a run on feed and this was the last they'd be seeing for quite a while. I was in no mood for their bullying and I upended their food onto the gravel yard before I was pecked to death. It was enough to give Tippi Hedren nightmares.

The female members of the brood, though, had had a record lay and their labours of love would go some way towards the bills. But all this didn't help my emotional state.

I debated whether to examine Stephanie's letters, which I'd slipped under the bed the previous night for safe-keeping. But really my heart wasn't in it. I had other, more pressing business with my lover.

I'd tracked Anne down to the spare bedroom and though it wasn't the first time she'd slept alone in recent months, I still found it hard to deal with. Her newly slim form was curled and vulnerable under the white summer-weight quilt. I didn't disturb her, though I felt maybe we should have that talk after all. Her clothes were strewn across the floor, I could almost follow her thought process as she'd disrobed. Shoes, black Nike pumps she'd taken to wearing, were kicked across the floor. Navy, figure-hugging pants were the next to go, turned inside-out in her haste to get to bed, ditto her limp white shirt. There was no sign of a bra and her knickers were under the bed.

Annoyed, but loving her, my brief desire for Stephanie was swept away under the deluge of feelings. So I tidied her clothes.

A crumpled note fell from her trousers: 'Now, we've all been here. To look or not to look, that is the question.'

I caught the beginnings of a local address, 23 Palm – before I screwed the paper up and shoved it back among her clothes. It was a decision I was to regret deeply.

The morning plodded on and I spent time weeding, fixing fences and generally putting into practice my farming skills.

It was after nine when Anne made an appearance. I shaded my eyes against the sun with my hand. Her figure cast a long shadow across the drive. 'Hi,' I said cheerfully, last night's irritation dissolving when I clapped eyes on her. 'You're late for work,' I pointed out.

She shrugged a 'who gives a toss?' kind of shrug. 'I'm taking the day off,' she called from the porch.

'Anything you want to do?' I asked, hoping for a trip into town, maybe to have a bite to eat in one of the bars on Canal Street. 'How does lunch in Manchester grab you?'

'Sorry, I've got meetings and things today. You know, about my book. I'm really too busy. And I've got some dry-cleaning to take in.'

Dry-cleaning? I don't think I'd ever heard her say those two words in all the years I'd known her.

'Anyway, isn't it the will today?' she asked.

'No,' I said. 'It's not till the end of the month.' Where

was her head to have forgotten something like that? I was unwilling to let the matter drop. 'I've got lots to tell you. There was that meeting with Stephanie for one thing – '

'Sorry, Letty, can it keep?' she interrupted. 'I've got such a lot to do today.'

'Okay,' I said, stung and a bit mystified. She was as wired as a cat at Crufts. 'Later then?'

'I'll see,' she murmured, checking her watch.

I made a show of hoeing the soil underfoot but kept one eye on Anne's fidgeting form. Suddenly she jumped off the porch and stumbled over to me. Flinging her arms around me, she kissed me on the mouth, almost hard enough to bruise me.

'Sorry,' she whispered, and before I could react she was marching quickly away, her car keys jangling in her hand.

'It's all right,' I shouted at her back. 'It doesn't matter,' I finished lamely. Though we both knew something did. 'I'll see you later then? Okay? Anne . . .' I called to her as her quick walk turned into a jog. 'Anne,' I yelled as she disappeared from view, but the sounds of her Ford Ka starting up drowned out the rest of my words.

She whipped the racy little motor from behind the back of the house. A couple of well-padded bin liners poked above the sill, partially blocking my view. Anne shot down the drive, gravel drumming under the wheel arches. She didn't look back.

'Was that Anne?' AnnaMaria asked from the kitchen door.

I jumped at her words. I was miles away.

'Yes. Have you spoken to her yet?'

'No. Her car woke me up. She's running a bit late, isn't she?'

'She's off work today. She's got her laundry to see to,' I snapped, suddenly angry.

'Her laundry? Letty, what are you talking about? Have you two had a row?'

I shook my head. 'No, it's just that things haven't been quite . . . ' I didn't finish the sentence. I didn't even want to think about it, never mind put it into words. 'I've just not had a chance to talk to her lately.' Or go out with her. Or have sex with her. Passion seemed to be a distant memory.

'She works too hard,' AnnaMaria offered. 'She's just tired. Anyway, Letty, the phone. It's for you.'

I chucked the hoe onto the ground and, stamping crusts of dry mud from my boots, went into the house.

AnnaMaria followed. 'It's your mother,' she whispered as I went for the receiver.

I had a quick, calming, Zen moment before speaking.

'Margaret,' I began carefully. 'How's Skegness?'

'Oh, the usual. Bracing as ever. Silly hats and chips with everything.' She laughed at her own description. 'I'm in Blackpool now,' she explained. 'I got bored with the east coast. It's probably time for home now.'

My mother was an elegant woman. Ageless, self-assured and a sucker for life's best offers. Her decision to visit Skegness via Scarborough instead of San Francisco (where my uncle, mentioned in Stephanie's letters, still lived) via Seattle had been a strange and as yet unexplained one. I suspected there was more to this than I would ever find out, but despite my questions, I knew she wasn't likely to give me a straight answer.

My mother and I loved each other dearly but had found that plenty of mileage between us made for a more harmonious relationship.

'What's wrong?' she asked.

'Nothing,' I said. 'You rang me, remember?'

'Letitia, I always know, even over the phone. How's Anne?' she added suddenly.

'Out.'

'Don't let it drag on,' she insisted, reading, somehow, a situation from eighty miles away.

'I won't, don't worry.' It had taken a good while for my mum to accept Anne. She'd always reckoned I could do better. 'Anyway, I'm glad you've rung. I need to speak to you. You're not on your mobile, are you?' I asked. She may still have had a good PA job, but with retirement less than a year away (though she'd been practising for that event for years) I didn't want her to chuck her money around.

'Goodness, no,' she replied breathlessly. 'I'm ringing from Blackpool. A mobile call would cost a fortune, especially the way you keep me talking.'

I began to protest at that outrageous suggestion but she cut me short. 'I'm ringing from the lobby phone at the hotel. It's on Cocker Street, behind the North Pier? It's such a beautiful place, run by two gay boys. You probably know them.'

I raised an eyebrow. My mother thought homosexuals had some strange cosmic link.

'What did you want to ask me?'

'It's a bit peculiar,' I began. 'So bear with me. It's about Cynthia.'

'Cynthia? My sister, Cynthia?'

'Yes. You know George's niece has turned up to sort out his belongings and stuff? And probably inherit the farm too. Well, some old letters of Cynthia's turned up – '

'Letitia,' she interrupted. Her voice had lost its chirpy tone and had instead taken on a very serious note, unheard of when she wasn't at work.

'What?'

'She found Cynthia's letters?' she asked quietly.

'Copies, at any rate.'

There was a long silence.

'Look, I'll be home in a day or two. Well, as soon as I can. I don't really want to talk about this on the phone. I'll speak to you when I get back. And not a word to anyone else. Promise me, Letitia.'

'Er, all right,' I stammered in agreement. 'You

obviously know more than me. I've not even read them yet.'

'It would be better if you never did,' Mum said, her voice suddenly cracking.

'Mum?' I said, alarmed. 'What's wrong?'

Over the airways I heard her discreetly blow her nose.

'I'll be fine,' she insisted. 'I'll come and see you as soon as I can. I have to go now,' she said abruptly.

'What did you call me about?' I didn't want her to hang up and distractions were more effective than demands as far as my mum was concerned.

'Nothing really, I just...' She paused. 'I was worried about you,' she said simply. 'And I really don't know why.'

'I'm fine,' I assured her. 'Come home soon, won't you?'

'Bye,' she said quietly, and the phone was replaced on the hook with a soft click.

'What the hell was that all about?' AnnaMaria asked from the kitchen.

'God knows,' I said. 'Mum being mysterious. She knows something about those letters. Honestly, they're making everybody crazy.'

'Well, go and get them then, and let's see what all the fuss is about,' AnnaMaria said, exasperated.

The expression on her face indicated that she would accept no arguments. Sighing, I went to the bedroom to get the letters.

I never got to them, not then anyway. An envelope lay on my pillow and across it, in Anne's familiar scrawl, was my name.

Chapter 19

I sat on the edge of the bed, all the breath gone from my body. It was impossible to ignore the letter, though I wished I'd never set eyes on it. A few years ago, even a few months ago, I would have snatched it up, expecting to get, if not exactly a love letter, a fun letter – a chatty note suggesting we were short of milk, or a promise of drinks later that evening.

This was saying things to me before I'd even ripped open the envelope. But I had to look.

Dear Letty,

I don't know how to start this letter. It is one of the most painful things I have ever done. 'I'm sorry' doesn't begin to express how I feel, and I can't expect either your understanding or your forgiveness. Maybe in time these things will be resolved, but for the moment I don't know how I can avoid hurting you, Letty.

My heart was cold with shock and the paper trembled in my hand. I read on until tears stopped me.

You've realised over the last few months that things haven't been right between us and, God knows, that's been my fault. If I'd had anything about me I would have ended it there, but I couldn't.

Letty, I've been seeing someone else and if that was all it was then I could have begged you for forgiveness. You've said yourself in the past that sometimes sex is all there is to a relationship. But this time there's more to it than that and the only honest thing I can do is leave.

I know I should have faced you with this and I've tried, believe me. I don't want to say who she is at the moment. You may even guess. Right now I just need space away until I sort myself out. Please try and understand me, though I know this letter has hardly explained anything. I'm sorry for the hurt this will cause, but please don't try and contact me. I will be in touch soon.

Please give the enclosed letter to AnnaMaria when she comes home.

Anne.

I sat clutching the sheet of paper for what seemed an age. If it hadn't been for AnnaMaria, I would still have been in the same position a week later.

'Letty, Letty,' she called as she bounded upstairs. 'Come on, slowcoach, before I die of curiosity.'

She burst into the bedroom, saw me, saw Anne's letter and immediately put two and two together. Anyone less astute would have had to ask.

She sat on the bed next to me and scanned the few pathetic words of explanation. 'Oh no. Oh, Letty,' she mumbled, wrapping her wiry arms around me.

She rocked me backwards and forwards. It didn't take long for my tears to soak through her T-shirt.

'I'm so sorry, Letty,' she whispered into my hair.

I couldn't speak and, after a while, I couldn't even cry.

'Letty, come on. You can't sit here all day. Let's go downstairs. Come on,' she urged, and she ushered me to my feet.

The kitchen looked the same as it had done an hour ago, but I knew there'd been some less than subtle shift and it was going to take a hell of a lot of adjustment not to see Anne in every corner.

Anne clutching a book; a pen; her niece's child. That soft and loving look was gone for good. I couldn't believe it, and I doubted then if I ever would.

AnnaMaria made a pot of tea as noisily as possible, while I sat on the settee staring into spaces Anne used to occupy. I could tell by the way AnnaMaria slammed about that she wanted to be seen to be angry, indignant even. Absolutely and utterly beside herself with rage. She was far angrier than me; the shock and hurt I felt would take a lot of replacing. And my own guilt was beginning to grow too. How could I have missed these signals? Why hadn't I tackled them before now? How could I possibly have let our relationship turn so bad, and not even try to sort it out? At what point did desire die for her? Just when had she had enough?

Clutching tea, AnnaMaria and I sat in silence. The world and my life had seemed so secure and safe. I was stunned how fast everything could change. And this was only the beginning. I had a feeling things would get a lot, lot worse.

Chapter 20

Later, as the news finally sank in, I asked AnnaMaria what her aunt had had to say to her. Her eyes had narrowed when she read her equally brief note, but she'd made no comment.

'Nothing much,' she said, scrubbing the sink as though her life depended on it. 'She's worried I'll be homeless,' she snapped.

'What?' I was astonished. Just what did Anne think I was?

AnnaMaria flung the sponge across the drainer. It bounced up and splattered against the window. I was glad it wasn't a scrubbing brush. Then she turned to face me. I'd never seen her so angry.

'Yeah, she thinks things might change now she's moved out and she's worried I won't have anywhere to go.' I was so astounded by this that for a moment I couldn't speak.

'You know I'd never do anything like that, don't you? I don't want you to leave. God, I won't *let* you leave. You're as much family as my mother is. I can't believe Anne didn't know me better than this,' I added with a whisper.

'I thought I knew her,' AnnaMaria said softly.

All the fight had suddenly gone from her voice. She took a seat at the kitchen table and reached for my hand. I squeezed her warm and damp fingers gently. This was painful for her too.

'Did she say anything about, you know?' I asked cautiously.

AnnaMaria found herself in a peculiar position. She knew I wanted to know about Anne's lover, though that thought made me feel physically sick. But she was a terrible liar and I'd know at once if she didn't tell me the truth.

'Yes, she did,' she said quietly. 'But I'm not going to tell you anything, Letty. Trust me, things are bad enough.'

I had to be satisfied with that and eventually, after more tears and angry words, AnnaMaria ordered me to bed. 'Just for an hour or two,' she suggested. 'You'll feel better, honest.'

'Well, I couldn't feel any worse,' I muttered. 'Though I don't know how I'll sleep. My mind just won't shut up.' And neither would my tears. Every now and again they'd come pouring, unbidden, from my eyes.

'Take this,' she ordered, and shoved a small white tablet into my hand. 'It'll help.'

I looked at it dubiously.

'It's herbal,' she explained.

'The hens?'

'Go to bed. I'll see to them,' and she shooed me upstairs.

Whatever the tablet was, it worked, and though I didn't feel much better when I woke up a few hours later, at least I didn't look as bad.

Julia was home when I staggered downstairs at five. She looked as shocked as I felt.

AnnaMaria was still banging about, but this time, having run out of pots to wash and sinks to clean, she was making tea. Pans full of vegetables were bubbling away on the Aga, the steam adding heat to the already hot and airless day.

'We're having cauliflower loaf and veggy burgers. Is that okay?'

My heart groaned in protest. The burgers had been for Anne. Something to put a little meat on her bones. She would be thin or fat without my help from now on.

'Fine,' I said.

'Letty,' Julia began, fidgeting at a distance. 'I don't know what to say. I'm sorry – '

I stopped her. 'It's all right. I don't want to talk about it.'

I was surprised, I really didn't want to talk about it. Not then, anyway. Maybe later, when drunkenness beckoned.

AnnaMaria had cooked a meal big enough for ten and, though I could only shuffle the food around my plate, I made an effort to eat just for her sake. The three of us had a blank couple of hours in front of the telly, and then the wine came out. And that's how the evening and the explanations began.

Chapter 21

'You might as well have shagged Stephanie then,' Julia ventured crudely as the alcohol took effect.

'Julia!' AnnaMaria growled from the kitchen sink, which she'd now decided to polish.

'It's all right,' I said distractedly, though shagging Stephanie was the last thing on my mind.

'Never even made it to the seven-year itch,' Julia went on in the same drunken vein.

Consideration of other people's feelings had never been her strong point.

'That's rich coming from you.' AnnaMaria leapt to my defence once more. 'Your relationships are classed as long term if they last seven weeks. Seven days sometimes,' she added.

'Please,' I said. 'That's enough.'

There was a lull for a moment as the television played to itself in the corner. AnnaMaria started work on an already spotless Aga.

'AnnaMaria,' Julia called. 'Come and join us, for God's sake. You've hardly sat down.'

'I'm too upset,' she confessed. 'I only came back to surprise Anne for her birthday. I've bought her this gorgeous swimming costume. She said she wanted one,' she added miserably. 'And now look what's happened.'

I'd bought her a rather magnificent watch some weeks earlier. What to do with it now? Smash the fucker with a hammer, that's what.

AnnaMaria turned to Julia, perfectly placed for her venom. 'And how do you think I feel, eh? She's my aunt, and I don't even know where she is, for Christ's sake.'

'Don't take it out on me,' Julia said defending herself. 'It's none of my doing.'

'Look,' I interrupted, too tired and too distraught to listen to the pair of them, 'it's not anybody's fault. It's not yours, it's not mine. It's not even Anne's. Things happen, things end.' I paused as Julia filled my glass.

The two women looked at me, as wary as speed freaks in a library.

'Don't look at me like that. I am not going to fall apart.' I was, however, going to get drunk and the wine, some trendy Napa Valley enamel-stripper Julia had bought, would do the trick nicely.

'AnnaMaria, please stop cleaning. You're as bad as Anne,' I said, and a great thumping solid golf ball of emotion lodged itself in my throat. Tears stung my eyes, sending the kitchen into strange and waterlogged 3D vision. I tried to blink the illusion away.

Julia, delving into herself to offer sympathy, patted my knee. AnnaMaria, rather more tactile, came over to hug me. Neither offered any words of comfort. Patting of knee and hugging of shoulders was more than enough to send me over the edge despite my earlier, brave words. I was prepared to allow myself only one night of public humiliation and this night with Julia, AnnaMaria and the Napa Valley wine would be it.

Finally, AnnaMaria relinquished her cloth and joined

us on the settee. She was not normally a wine drinker but, short of anything more agreeable, she took the glass on offer.

'Jesus wept!' she spluttered after the first taste. 'What's this crap? Best buy at Kwiksave?'

'Expert now, are we?' Julia happily rose to the occasion. It was far easier to bicker with AnnaMaria than try to deal with my love life. I would have exchanged places any day. But eventually, shit-faced after a long evening of excess and with Julia pulling out all the stops to entertain me with stories past, present and imaginary, the world didn't seem so bad.

'I won't see her, never, ever,' I said on Napa Valley night. 'I don't need her,' I mumbled through tears that made a mockery of my words.

AnnaMaria hugged me some more. Julia opened yet another bottle of wine and put jolly songs on the CD player. I wanted angst: a forlorn Julia Fordham; a morose Melissa Etheridge; Tanita Tickaram with toothache; the Walker Brothers a-weeping and a-wailing because the sun had gone in for good. And what did I get? The Spice Girls. Rich, famous and around long enough to make a best-of album.

I went to bed about three and despite the acres of farmhouse space available now that I was alone (more tears, more golf balls in the throat), I ended up with AnnaMaria sprawled asleep across the bottom of the bed.

My friends didn't let me out of their sight.

Until the day she came back.

She came back.

But not for me.

Chapter 22

I spent a miserable week, the hottest of the summer in fact, gardening, collecting eggs and tending a new brood of chickens blossoming in the midsummer sun. Idyllic, you'd think, except for the hours spent nursing a broken heart that had been chewed up and spat out.

Unconcerned, to any great extent, I'd watched the odd comings and goings at George's farm. Occasionally Stephanie made an appearance and she'd waved, but hadn't come over. I was glad. Her occasional phone calls, sometimes answered, sometimes avoided, and the woman herself, were a distraction I didn't think I needed. The only conversation that had stuck in my mind was the strange and unexplained information that George's will-reading had been put back a couple of weeks. Even the letters she'd entrusted me with were unread and gathering dust under the bed.

AnnaMaria managed to catch Mum on her mobile to explain what had happened. Despite our bizarre and as yet untackled phone call, so far she'd managed to keep her distance. But I couldn't hide for ever, and AnnaMaria couldn't protect me for ever either. Not having Liam around, she was already battling with her own missing link and the day she'd chosen to return to Italy was drawing near. I would have to face things alone sooner or later. Julia, being Julia, was sympathetic at first, though my mopings were beginning to test her will-power.

'Have you tried to ring her?' she asked me as I struggled with the garden one too-bright day.

'How?' I snapped. 'I don't even know where she is. Anne wasn't exactly forthcoming, was she?'

Against my better judgement, I'd shown Anne's extraordinarily out of character letter to Julia. She'd gone through it with more insight than I would have given her credit for. And more understanding of my ex-partner's motives than I would ever have expected. Not that I was prepared to listen.

'Despite words to the contrary, she's trying to shift the blame. Don't you see?' she began a couple of days after the Napa valley.

Julia had come home for lunch and had joined me in my misery on the porch. With her camel-coloured lightweight suit and brown leather briefcase, she didn't look an ideal candidate for sunbathing on a West Yorkshire chicken farm.

'No.'

Julia, ignoring my obstinacy, managed to keep her patience. 'Look,' she went on. 'All this crap about sexual relationships, words you are supposed to have said. Well, I'm sorry, Letty, but if I'm to be brutally honest that's more likely to be something *I'd* say.'

'Julia, is this supposed to make me feel better?'

'Letty, you're not listening to me. She's passing the buck. She can't cope with hurting you, so, in a round-about way, she's trying to ease her conscience. Especially considering the new light of her life,' she added brightly.

I sat up quickly. 'What do you know?' I snapped.

'Julia!' AnnaMaria, eavesdropping from the front door, shouted angrily. 'Your mouth will get you into so much trouble one of these days! Letty,' she went on, 'I told her about my letter too. I'm sorry. She was sworn to secrecy.' She glared at an uncomfortable Julia.

'So . . .' I said.

'So what?' Julia looked puzzled.

'It's her agent,' AnnaMaria interrupted. 'Debbie Jones.'

I sighed, envisioning the woman. Tall and tanned and lovely . . . yeah, and the rest. A couple of years my junior and a salary light years away from my own.

'Great,' I whispered. 'What else did she say? Apart from thinking I'd make you homeless.'

'There you are!' Julia said triumphantly. 'Another case of misplaced guilt.'

'Julia, please! No more of your pop psychology. Wait till I'm drunk again.' There was a moment before I asked, 'How long has she been seeing her?'

'Letty, I'm not getting involved in this,' AnnaMaria had insisted. 'You'll have to ask her yourself.'

I would have if I could have found her.

'Have you tried the library?' Julia pressed. Thankfully, she'd abandoned her therapy sessions after that last conversation. 'Surely they'll know where she is.'

I sighed. 'Well, if they do, they're not saying. You know what they can be like. "I'm sorry, Ms Campbell, but we're not at liberty to disclose her whereabouts. Miss Marple made it quite clear that her four-week vacation was not to be disturbed. On any account,"' I said mimicking, badly, the head of personnel's Scottish accent.

'Can't you say it's a family crisis?'

'It is,' I pointed out.

'Wouldn't they tell AnnaMaria?'

'No! I won't use her as a go-between. I doubt if she'd let me anyway.'

'What about Mrs Buckham?'

I looked at her in miserable surprise. 'Why would they tell her anything?'

'Oh, come on, Letty. She could get a confession from the Pope.'

I'd already had Sylvia on the phone, offering commiserations, advice, even money, but no explanation as to how she'd found out. I'd managed to fob her off temporarily, though it wouldn't be long before she was knocking on my door.

'So what are you going to do then?' She couldn't entirely hide the irritation in her voice.

'I am going to go on digging this fucking trench, if that's all right. Then I'm going to feed the fucking chickens. And then,' I said, slamming the spade into a particularly unyielding lump of earth, 'I'm going to get drunk, again!'

'I only asked,' Julia muttered nervously.

'Well, don't,' I growled. 'If you're fed up, go back to work, or go home, or whatever.'

'I can't,' she said, missing the point altogether. 'My friends are using the flat. They're staying the summer, remember? Anyway, the competition's been delayed. There's been a technical hitch.'

I couldn't help but laugh at that. 'A technical hitch? In darts?!'

Julia looked relieved. Laughter she could deal with. 'I know, crazy, isn't it?'

The sound of rubber tyres on the gravel drive attracted my attention. A two-year-old Vauxhall Tigra, the colour of newly set sticky toffee, pulled up outside the house.

Julia and I looked questioningly at the strange vehicle. And then Anne stepped out of the passenger door.

'I'll go and, er,' Julia mumbled, and headed for the house.

The two women exchanged wary nods as they passed

116

each other. Heart thundering, I looked beyond Anne to see who had been driving the car. The tinted windows revealed nothing.

Anne looked different somehow. Fitter, younger even. Her hair had been cut short and dyed a darker shade. Her clothes were new and stylish. For Christ's sake, she even looked taller. Sunglasses hid her eyes. Who was this stranger before me?

She turned to the car and signalled... What? That her companion should stay in the car? That she was okay? In any case, no one ventured from behind the wheel.

Anne crunched her way across the gravel and stood facing me. The two feet between us might as well have been two miles.

'Letty,' she acknowledged.

I was suddenly aware of my appearance. Grubby, sweaty and unkempt would have been a kindly description.

'Anne,' I said, 'how are you?' Stupid really, she was obviously fine. 'Have you come...' I paused as the words threatened to drift away. 'Have you come to talk?' I asked finally.

She looked beyond me. Even from behind coloured glass, it was evident she couldn't bear to look me in the face.

'No,' she said quietly, but with some hint of defiance in her voice. 'I was going to ring. I've come for a few things.'

There, it was said. I waited to die at her feet.

'I didn't think you'd be here.'

'Anne.' A note of pleading crept into my voice and I clutched the spade for support. 'Anne, where else would I be?'

'I'm sorry' she said, biting her bottom lip. A familiar gesture, one she used in bed. One I knew I would never see again, not like that. 'I know how you must feel.'

'No, you don't!' I said bitterly, fighting back tears.

'You've no idea how I feel. How could you?'

I moved towards her, the anger I'd been fighting roaring forth from some inner depth. She took a step back; perhaps she thought I was going to finish her off with the spade.

'Not a word. Not a fucking word! You left me a note. YOU LEFT ME A NOTE. After six years, six fucking years, you left me a note! And I'm supposed to be okay about that?'

I suddenly laughed at her, an incredulous, unbelieving and gleeful sound, like Jack Nicholson in *The Shining*. She stepped back again. 'And now you tell me you know how I feel? Well, whoopee-fucking-do.'

Suddenly reaching up, I ripped her sunglasses off her face. I wouldn't, no, I couldn't let her hide behind them. Control was slipping away faster than the tide at Southport.

'Letty, please,' she said, panic replacing the defiance in her voice. 'I'm sorry, but I couldn't face you. Your hurt, your anger, the way you might react...'

'*Coward*,' I spat. 'And what a note you left me.' I'd memorised the words. I felt as though it would be years before I could erase them. 'So you just tell me, now. Look me in the eye and *tell me*,' I roared.

AnnaMaria, doing an oil change on my Land Rover at the other side of the house, and alerted by raised voices, came rushing around the corner. She skidded to a halt when she saw Anne.

'Well?' I said.

My body was shaking but, wanting an answer, I wouldn't let go of this. Anne looked at me then, a sad and serious look on her face. And I knew. I knew before she even spoke.

'It's over for me, Letty. There are other things in my life, other directions I need to – '

'Spare me,' I said, exhaustion suddenly taking over

where anger had left off. A cold and bitter feeling filled the space where my heart used to be. 'One thing. Why didn't you tell me about her?'

Her startled look made me even sadder. She looked away then, back towards the car. A figure stepped out. Debbie, of course.

'Are you all right, Anne?' she called, genuine concern in her voice.

Anne nodded. 'I won't be a minute.'

A minute. For six years. Not much of an exchange.

I turned away, dragging the spade with me. 'Get what you need,' I said tiredly. 'I've not touched anything.'

I wandered past a worried AnnaMaria, who stroked my shoulder briefly. Caught between a rock and a hard place, she dithered.

'Go and talk to her,' I said. 'Make sure she's all right,' I added with a shudder.

'If you're sure?'

I waved her away. I had to move on and now was as good a time to start as any.

Chapter 23

'You need a distraction,' Julia declared with the air of a woman who had just discovered the meaning of life.

'You reckon?' I replied as I stared after an Air2000 plane bound for even hotter climes than those Britain was alternately loving and loathing.

We were at the airport, seeing AnnaMaria off for a second time. The day had finally arrived when she had to go back to Milan. Desire for Liam's company was so strong it was coming off her in waves. I could empathise with that. Missing someone was a concept I was getting to grips with.

Anne had made a further trip to the farm. The last of her belongings were duly collected, but in my absence. I'd wandered down to the bottom fields as she'd packed, with only twenty-five sheep for company (a neighbour from the other side of the valley was renting my spare land for grazing purposes). I didn't trust myself to be near her. I had no idea how I'd react and I wasn't particularly keen to find out. Sadness and anger had become intermingled, so much so that I could barely tell them apart. I wasn't sure whether I wanted to beg her to stay or scream abuse at her. I even wanted to scream abuse at the sheep. White-faced and knock-kneed, the flock of identical animals bleated their dismal and unreadable message, the sound matching my mood perfectly.

AnnaMaria's relationship with my former lover was even more complicated. She'd done her best not to take sides and had striven not to be judgemental. An heroic effort for anyone in the circumstances.

AnnaMaria had found out that her aunt was living only a few miles away, in a rented cottage in the nearby village of Langton and not in some lovenest with her new woman. Stupidity was not something Anne suffered from.

'Look,' Julia said, nudging me away from these difficult memories, 'that's AnnaMaria's plane.'

A British Airways Boeing 737 eased onto the runway, its powerful turbo engines loud enough to echo through the reinforced windows of the viewing lounge. We waved furiously, knowing AnnaMaria couldn't see us.

The plane was a small dot in the distance when Julia suggested we have a coffee. Manchester Airport was one of her favourite places. I knew we'd go back loaded down with pamphlets and travel brochures, and the business of planning a holiday for Julia next year would begin.

'Las Vegas, now there's a place,' she said, staring at a poster on the café wall. I looked at the shot of the sprawling metropolis. It looked false, fabricated and fun.

'You've not been before, have you?' I asked her as she lit a cigarette.

'Sadly, no,' she replied, looking for an ashtray. She ignored or was oblivious to, the no-smoking sign almost above her head. She decided to use her saucer as an ashtray. 'It's a thought for next year, though, don't you think?'

I shrugged.

'You could come too,' she offered. 'We'd have a great time.'

Keeping Julia out of jail when she thought she'd been cheated on the roulette wheel would probably occupy me, I thought with a grimace.

American voices, oddly, surrounded us. Students from Chicago, judging by their Illinois accent, were sat at tables nearby. Wealthy American students too, by the looks of them. Their clothes were ghetto chic. Tommy Hilfiger primary colours nudging Levi's into second place. Even their rucksacks were immaculate. Not the usual and functional ex-army-store luggage favoured by poorer travellers.

'So, what's the distraction you've got in mind then?'

Julia dumped her cigarette into the remains of her coffee.

'How can people drink this muck,' she grumbled quietly.

'Julia?' I pressed.

She looked up and held my gaze with those impossibly grey eyes. She grinned broadly. 'Shopping.'

'Oh, Julia, for God's – '

'Let me finish,' she said. 'Sooner or later you're going to want to re-enter society,' she went on in her own heavy-handed way. 'You think your farm holds all the delights you'll ever need. Well, it doesn't. There is a world out there, you know? So come on. Sup up and shut up,' she ordered, pushing her coffee cup to one side. Sighing, I followed her lead.

Chapter 24

'The first thing we have to do,' Julia began as we scoured the short-stay car park looking for her new MGF convertible, 'is – ' she stopped as her latest toy eluded her for a moment. 'We are on Level 3?' she asked as she examined her ticket.

'Yes,' I replied, looking around for her little red sports car.

Despite her constant moaning about the state of her finances, she (or possibly her mother) had finally fought off the shackles of co-owning a car with AnnaMaria. One day Julia's dream of driving around in a Ferrari would be realised, but for the moment her MG was enough of a head turner – a stomach churner, the way Julia handled the horsepower that lurked under the bonnet.

'Here we are,' she said with some relief as the jewel in her crown turned up tucked away between a Jag and a Jeep. 'The first thing we have to do,' she repeated, firing the engine, 'is to find some decent shops.'

I was far too sad to be offended, and concentrated instead on squeezing my body into the little bucket seat.

Julia threw a switch and the electrically operated soft top folded itself neatly at the rear of the car. The device had been fitted at her own expense, for an amount that would have secured a second car, or the deposit on a small house. 'A snip,' she'd insisted, ignoring the look of shock on my face, and the 'you've been done' curl that had appeared on AnnaMaria's lip.

The car park's strip-lighting illuminated my plain blue jeans and slightly weary white T-shirt.

'Why do I need new clothes?' I asked. 'And if you say I need them for a woman who hasn't even entered my life yet, I'll brain you.'

'What sort of insensitive creature do you take me for?' Julia asked, reversing out of the parking place at speed. My guts stayed in the parking space. She rammed the little car into first and we had a few nail-biting minutes as we headed down the ramps. We finally hit the less than choked M56, where Julia slotted the car into the middle lane and we were soon doing eighty, but heading in completely the opposite direction of where I wanted to go.

'Julia,' I yelled over the screaming air tunnel our speed was creating, 'where the hell are we going?'

'Wait and see,' she shrieked in response.

There were no other attempts at conversation. The MG's CD player, miniaturised and state of the art, was more than a match for Britain's ill-maintained motorways and Vanessa Mae's soaring violin filled any potential conversational gaps.

Thirty minutes later both of us looking like the straw man, we pulled up at Cheshire Oaks Retail Village, on the outskirts of Chester, home to designer clothes at bargain-basement prices. Searching for a parking space, Julia suddenly slammed her foot on the brake. My seat belt kicked in, holding me firmly against the upholstery. 'I know that car,' Julia said, pointing to a similar, but much older, model to her own. 'Never forget one of those,' she mumbled. 'Especially if I'm the one who sold it.'

The chunky little sportster was in good, if not pristine, condition.

'Who did you sell it to?' I asked a thoughtful Julia.

'Mmm, Ruth I think she was called. Yes, Ruth, definitely Ruth. I can't recall her last name offhand. She was the one who didn't haggle over the price, remember?'

'Vaguely,' I said, still breathless after the journey.

'Oh, well. It's bound to turn up somewhere, I suppose. There aren't that many around.'

She found a space of her own and slotted her MG neatly into place.

'Julia, this isn't fair,' I grumbled, climbing out of the car and rubbing the knots from my muscles. 'I'm not in the mood for shopping. It might solve all your problems, but it doesn't solve mine.'

'Oh, shut up,' she said good-naturedly as she secured the car. 'Half an hour isn't going to kill you. Besides, you need something new for Saturday.'

'Saturday? Why?' I asked suspiciously.

'We're going out. Scrub that. Sita and I are taking you out. You've got two choices. Dinner and a club. There's a fabulous new place in town called Dusty's, a new venue for dykes like us.'

'Like us?'

'For anybody over nineteen,' she explained, un-comfortably acknowledging her older-dyke status. I didn't feel older. I had as much control over my life at the moment as a twelve-year-old.

'Or we could have dinner and a trip to the pictures. Either will be fun. Listen and learn from your dearest friend.'

'I don't fancy either,' I grumbled.

'Then the pictures it is,' she decided.

*

125

Her shopping therapy proved to be more successful than the other regimes she'd tried to impose.

It took a lot longer than her predicted half an hour to get me kitted out, but after an initial 'I don't care what I look like' moan, she'd persuaded me into some clothes that were very swish indeed.

'Velvet. Blue velvet. You'd look sensational in that,' she insisted as we prowled around the shops.

'Julia, it's in the eighties, remember?' I said as we sweated.

'Well, it's not going to be like this for ever, is it? Anyway, these are all last season's clothes. You didn't expect summer wear, did you?'

Julia found a thigh-length velvet jacket which, when it didn't fit her, she forced on me.

'Thirty quid. A bargain. I'll treat you,' she offered, while I debated.

'No, you won't. But I will buy it,' I said almost to myself. It was a stunning item, and one day, when the weather was cold and my heart was warmer, I knew I would wear it too.

She dragged me into Next after that and we found a blouse to go with it.

'Trousers, trousers,' Julia mumbled as she disappeared among racks of clothing. 'Chino's' she announced. 'You can't go wrong in these.' They were soft moleskin and I couldn't resist adding them to my shopping basket.

'A whole new outfit for under seventy quid,' Julia crowed, as we sat outside a café nursing orange juice an hour later.

The other shoppers were as languid as us, the heat too intense for anything other than cold drinks and quiet conversation. Julia slipped a pair of dark glasses on. She could have been at Cannes.

'Have you heard from Sita?' I asked, for her lover had been in London for a while now.

126

She pushed her glasses up onto her head. Definitely Cannes.

'She's fine,' she said and looked around at the other overheated shoppers. 'She told me she loved me before she went away,' she added quietly.

Her face was serious. This was a big deal for Julia. Relationships were common, sex was even commoner, but love, for Julia, was a rarity. I pushed away my own feelings of loss before I could comment.

'And how do you feel?'

'I want to be with her so badly, I almost ache,' she said simply.

I wished I had a pair of sunglasses to cover my own eyes. Tears flooded them before I could do anything about it.

Julia reached for my hand. 'Oh, I'm sorry, Letty. That was totally unfeeling of me.'

'It's all right,' I said, sniffing. 'I'm glad you told me. I like Sita,' I managed, stopping the flood of feelings before I made a complete fool of myself. I tried to smile. 'Any plans?' I ventured, as I got myself under control again.

'Such as?'

'Living together, running off into the sunset together, buying a cottage in Wales?' I asked, my smile a little broader. A little more genuine.

'No need for all that,' she said. 'We already live in the same apartment block. Why spoil a good thing?' Julia uttered the cautious words I'd been expecting, but then she suddenly leaned closer, the sunglasses back in place. 'Don't look now,' she whispered, 'but about three tables behind you there is a very familiar figure indeed.'

'Not Anne?' I asked, panic-stricken.

'No!' Julia hissed. She flapped her hands dismissively at my suggestion. 'Hi,' she said over my shoulder a moment later.

I looked around and a pair of friendly green eyes looked into mine.

'Julia,' Stephanie said in that deep voice I remembered so well. 'And Letty, how wonderful to see you again. May I join you for a moment?'

'Of course,' I said, and moved a chair out for her.

'I'm sorry...' we said in unison, and we laughed a little uncomfortably.

Julia stood up to go and get fresh drinks.

'So,' Stephanie began, 'I've not seen much of you.'

In deference to the weather, she was wearing green, almost military-cut shorts and a loose white shirt. She was more tanned than I remembered, though her hair was in its usual brushed-back style.

I was at a loss. Despite our spasmodic telephone conversations, she knew nothing, as far as I was aware, of recent developments. How could I even begin to tell this woman, who was still almost a stranger, what had been happening to me?

She saved me the effort.

'I heard what happened. I'm sorry. If you need anything?'

I held up my hand. She made it sound as though there had been a death in the family, and in a way I suppose there had. I certainly felt bereaved.

'Who told you?' I asked, dreading it would be Julia.

'Mrs Buckham,' Stephanie explained, laughing gently. 'Are you okay?'

I rocked my hand. So-so.

'I know this may be an inappropriate time, but have you looked at your Aunt Cynthia's letters yet?'

'I've not really felt like it, to be honest. One thing, though, I did mention them to my mum. She seemed a bit concerned. In fact, she seemed to have some idea what they were about. More than me at any rate.'

Stephanie looked at her hands and rubbed them slowly together; the rasp of skin against skin reminded me of our other, slightly chilling, conversation. And although in one way I felt that our encounter had taken place ten years ago, somehow her actions made me recall the way we'd said goodbye.

'Perhaps we should go through them together? I think it's time we had a look, don't you think?'

I sat back and studied the woman for a moment, my thoughts and feelings in confusion.

'Tonight?' I suggested, finally. 'Come for tea. We could go through them afterwards. Maybe even solve the mystery.' The prospect of spending a night with something other than Anne's ghost was very appealing.

'Fine with me. Is seven-thirty okay?'

I nodded and smiled. 'I've seen you at the farm a few times. What have you got in mind? Are you going to renovate it?'

'It's too early to tell. Officially, I don't even know that I can do anything with it yet,' she said.

'Surely it's just red tape now?'

She shrugged. 'Hopefully, though the police report still hasn't come through. We do have contact with George's solicitors now. Ruth Smedley, one of the partners, is a close friend of my family. Of course, she can't tell me anything, but...in fact she's here with me today. I think I've lost her in one of the shops,' she said with a wry smile.

I remembered Julia's remarks about Richardson and Smedley. It was still a bit odd to think of old George having anything to do with the likes of them. Money stashed under his mattress would have been more his style. I found it hard to imagine him forking out for their services. But there was obviously a lot I didn't know, and probably would never know, about the old man.

'Anyway, I'd better get going and find Ruth. I want to be home when my husband gets there.'

The faintest cloud had crossed her forehead with these words. I doubted she even realised. I got up with her and, not knowing whether to hug her or shake her hand, I did neither, just waved her off.

Julia came back after a few minutes, clutching a tray and a bag.

'Has she gone?' she asked. 'And what did Stephanie "did anybody notice I'm loaded?" Evershaw-Adam have to say?'

I laughed aloud at Julia's cutting remark. A few lethargic heads turned my way.

'Careful,' Julia said. 'You'll wake the dead.'

'Looks like hubby insists she's home when he's finished doing whatever it is he does all day.'

'I thought you said she worked.'

'She does. Supply lecturer or whatever they're called. She turns up when they need her.'

'They don't need her at the moment?'

'Just for the odd summer lecture,' I explained.

Julia sucked her teeth. 'It's him. I told you he was strange. Charming but strange. I don't understand why she's with him. He was at least twenty years older. Dominating, I bet, but . . .'

'Julia!' I laughed. 'You've only met him once.'

'Letty, my love, once was more than enough. Didn't anybody tell her women have the vote now?'

'Didn't anybody tell him?' I said, taking her observations at face value.

'He told me what he did for a living, you know,' she explained.

'Oh yeah?'

'You're not going to like it.'

'So don't tell me then.'

'He's a property developer,' she went on, ignoring my suggestion.

'So?'

'Letty, think!' she ordered. 'Who's in line for George's farm, mmm?'

'Julia, it's a farm. In the middle of West Yorkshire. It's

uses must be a bit limited. It's not like the bloody by-pass they threatened us with a couple of years ago,' I reminded her, alluding to a particularly messy period of our lives. 'It's agricultural land. There must be laws.'

'Look, I'm just telling you, that's all. You know how you worry.'

'By the way,' I said, more than happy to change a subject I didn't want to think about. 'Did you sell that MG to a Ruth Smedley.'

'Yeah, that's her. How do you know?'

'Apparently she's a friend of Stephanie's.'

'And George's solicitor?' she suddenly added as light dawned. 'Curious.'

'Or dodgy. It depends how you look at it.'

'Letty, I never thought I'd meet someone more suspicious than AnnaMaria. I got that wrong,' she said with a smile.

'Misery does strange things,' I muttered.

'Anyway, never mind all that. Here, these are for you,' and she handed me her package.

Julia on occasion, was as considerate to me as anyone had ever been in my life, though less consistently than Anne. That thought gave me the sweetest, saddest and loneliest kind of pain I could ever imagine. I stamped hard on my feelings before they could affect my tear ducts again. This had to stop.

'Aren't you going to look then?' she asked. Over the years I'd spent a couple of Christmases with Julia and, like my mum with literature, surprise was not something she relished. She'd marvelled at my ability not to rip open every present dotted around the long-suffering plastic Christmas tree before the designated day. When I'd demanded the same of her, well, her tantrums surpassed even Liam's when denied a second helping of pudding.

Remembering all this, I opened my present. A set of underwear lay among the delicate tissue paper and silk ribbons. I read the label, for with Julia there had to be one. Dolce & Gabbana, the familiar black initials tastefully interwoven in the waistband of the knickers and the supporting elastic of the bra.

'I guessed your size,' Julia said, oblivious to the intimacy of her purchase.

Tears stabbed at the back of my throat and it was a full minute before I could thank her.

Julia beamed. She liked to be appreciated.

'Anyway, are you ready to go? If you leave the chickens any longer, they'll be ringing the RSPCA.'

I laughed, wondering and pleased at my ability to do so twice within an hour, and followed her to the car.

Chapter 25

One thing a day out and a set of new clothes did for me was to prompt a general spring-clean. Anne was gone. She was not going to come back. Time to clear her out.

Easier said than done, of course. I had two hours before Stephanie was due. Time enough at least to do the bedroom.

If Anne had found that writing a letter to tell me our relationship was finished was the hardest thing she'd ever done, well, clearing out six years of memories was the most difficult for me. I resisted the temptation of looking through every photo ever taken. Instead, I locked them in an old metal chest and chucked the key down the toilet. That action seemed to say a great deal.

Anne had already taken most of her stuff, but the odd garment still remained under the bed, behind the wardrobe or lurking at the back of a drawer. I binned them all.

I moved the bed against a different wall, knowing it would take me days to get used to the new position, but the odd sleepless night was nothing new. I retrieved

Stephanie's dusty letters and put them to one side for later. The curtains were removed and thrown in the wash, and a spare blind was put up somewhat crookedly in their place. Made of untreated calico, the blind let in a soft, diffused light. With a new quilt cover I'd bought that day, the bedroom looked completely different. I would decorate soon, I decided. But for the moment the spring-clean would have to do.

And me? I was coping, and that was enough.

'What time is she coming?' Julia asked.

'Half-past seven.'

'Do you want me out of the way?'

I thought for a moment. 'Do you mind?'

'No. Cool,' she said. 'I'll ring the girls at home. They owe me a night out. What exactly does Stephanie want to see you about?'

Julia had managed to stamp on her curiosity, but the cracks in her resolve were beginning to show.

'I'll tell you tomorrow,' I offered. 'When I know more myself.'

'Promise?'

I nodded.

'Okay. I'll be off then and let you get on with your little mysteries. And don't do anything I wouldn't do,' she suggested as she grabbed her car keys and made for the door.

I refused to answer her corny remark with a worse one of my own, tempting as it was. 'Bye, Julia,' was all I said as she slammed out of the back door.

I didn't let the house descend into silence. Rod Stewart was an odd choice for me, but his mid-Atlantic sing-a-long-a-twang filled every corner of my farmhouse as I clattered about cooking vegetable lasagne. I was slaughtering 'Maggie May' when I heard an insistent knock on the door.

Clutching two bottles of wine, Stephanie stepped into my steamy kitchen.

'This okay?' she asked, shoving one of the bottles of Frascati in my hands.

'Is it alcoholic?' I asked with a smile.

She laughed. 'Oh yes. Twelve and a half per cent, and a very good year.'

'I don't care if it was bottled yesterday,' I offered, suddenly and pleasantly at ease with her.

'I'd better pour it then, before it gets too old,' and she retrieved two glasses from the pine sideboard. 'A fan of Rod Stewart, are you?' she asked as she poured the pale and obviously chilled wine.

'Maggie May' had been replaced by the embarrassingly inappropriate, 'Tonight's the Night'.

'Cleaning music,' I explained with a smile as I took the glass from her. 'Change it if you want.'

'God, no!' she said. 'I loved the Seventies. I was young, free, single and living abroad then.'

She took a seat at the table as I pottered around the Aga. I could feel her eyes on the back of my neck. For one wild moment I hoped it was clean. 'Where were you?'

'Oh, various places. My stepfather was in the forces. He was a diplomat in the Navy. He met my mother years after the war. He died with her in a boating accident. Ironic, isn't it?'

Ironic isn't necessarily the word I would have used. But who was I to judge?

'Did your uncle ever know about it?' I asked.

'No, he and Mary, my mother, hadn't been in touch for years. They didn't really get on.'

I pondered this and mentally tried to sort her family tree into some semblance of order.

'When I was younger we never stayed anywhere for long. We were in Dresden for the longest time, though Lucerne was always my favourite. The climate, the colleges, the art galleries, the architecture. It was a fabulous place to be.'

I couldn't begin to compete with that. Skegness and Cleethorpes wouldn't impress her, and Hallway Secondary School for Girls, Greater Manchester's last outpost in the education department, didn't exactly ring bells where achievements were concerned. I'd left there clutching a couple of 'O' levels and a commendation for my hockey skills.

'Where were you educated?' she asked innocently.

I could have made something up, I suppose. But borrowing Julia's past (even though I knew it was better than my own) would have been a shallow thing to do. So I told her the truth. I thought she wouldn't be impressed, but she was interested and there are always little stories to tell. Mistakenly, I doubted if she had encountered stink bombs thrown during morning service. Or public canings in front of the whole school. Nowadays it sounds like something from Dickens. But I was wrong. She didn't only match my anecdotes, she bettered them. Her tales of grand auto theft were nothing compared to the kidnapping of the headmistress.

'I wasn't involved, of course,' she said slyly, more than a twinkle flickering in her eye. 'But it certainly caused some trouble.'

We shared more wine and stories from the past as the lasagne bubbled away in the oven. It was obvious we were as different from each other as Prince Philip and a Greek wine waiter, but we enjoyed each other's company.

It took a few seconds to do something creative with a side salad and then I asked her about her husband, swivelling from my position at the sink in time to see those long lashes close momentarily over her remarkable eyes. 'Ah, Claude,' she said.

'You were married recently? Is that right?' I asked, dishing out the dinner.

'Married recently? Yes. In fact – ' she paused. 'In fact, Claude is my stepfather's son.'

I already knew that piece of information, supplied by Anne a thousand years ago. 'Oh,' was all I said.

'Don't worry,' she said with a smile, 'it is legal.'

'I don't suppose I need to ask how you met then?'

She laughed, a relieved sort of laugh, as I presented her with her meal.

'Oh, lasagne. Wonderful,' she said.

I peered at the sloppy mess on her plate. I sincerely hoped it tasted better than it looked.

We got stuck in and it hit me that I'd not thought about Anne for at least an hour. Things were looking up.

Now Stephanie was skinny, there's no getting around that, and her close-fitting jeans and ribbed T-shirt did nothing to disguise the fact. But she quickly and rather delicately cleared her plate and ate most of the salad. I had an uncomfortable thought about bulimia, but that skin and those sparkling eyes were far too healthy for that sort of ailment. Obviously she had the same metabolic rate as AnnaMaria. I, on the other hand, was still struggling with an appetite that had sneaked out through the back door.

Stephanie poured more wine. 'Aren't you hungry?' she asked with some concern.

I pulled a face in response. She seemed to get the message.

'Do you want to talk about it?'

I began to say no, and then it all came flooding out. It was easy, probably too easy, to tell this woman how I felt. She didn't take sides and offered no easy answers, just support and, at some point during the outpouring, her hand.

I waited for warning signals from my brain, but there didn't seem to be any. And it was the most natural thing in the world when she leaned across the table to kiss me.

I never thought I'd want to kiss anyone again, but when Stephanie's warm, full mouth settled on mine, I couldn't think of anything I'd rather be doing.

But it was she who pulled back.

'That was unfair of me,' she said, her eyes skittering away, refusing to focus on anything but the table top.

'Unfair to whom?' I asked. Her good education and perfect grammar were catching.

She smiled and looked at me. 'You, me, probably others if I thought about it long enough.'

I didn't want to think. I wanted to do.

'It's a bit sudden,' I managed and then laughed, again.

Stephanie looked surprised and then laughed too. She was still holding my hand and she caressed it gently. We had to start something or stop altogether.

'I'll get those letters,' I offered. 'While I still can.'

'Wait,' she said. 'Please, Letty.' She got up, pulling me gently with her. There was no thought, no awkwardness, and she drew me into her arms and kissed me again. Desire was like a punch in the stomach. Breathless, she said. 'Take me to bed.'

I didn't even hesitate.

Later, when I'd retrieved the rest of the wine from the kitchen, I asked Stephanie a question that had been on my mind.

'Why did you get married?' I laughed awkwardly. 'You're not new to this.'

She sat up and took the glass on offer. The quilt, tucked across her breasts, dwarfed her small frame. She shrugged and pushed her seriously disarrayed hair from her face.

'I don't sleep with Claude. It's not that sort of relationship.'

'Then why . . . ?'

'Questions, questions,' she said, smiling. 'Letty, I really don't want to talk about it. We go our own way, that's all you need to know. Claude really wouldn't care about this at all. I don't want you to worry about it.'

I didn't, that was the strange thing, though extramarital affairs weren't something I was particularly familiar with. Seconds ticked by.

'Is this a one-off?' I asked, needing to know what she felt.

'Is that what you want?' she threw back.

I didn't answer, because I had a feeling it probably was. She'd made me feel desirable and I suspected I didn't have a need for anything more than that.

She smiled and took my glass from my hand.

Well, maybe more than just once then.

Chapter 26

'On your own then?' Julia yelled cheerfully the following morning.

'Mmm,' I said, opening one eye. 'Time?'

'Seven-forty-five. Time you were up.'

'Run the shower,' I ordered, rubbing my face.

My fingers brushed against my lips and I was jolted fully awake by memories. I sat up quickly. A note was on the pillow next to me. I grabbed the piece of paper and shoved it under the quilt before Julia spotted it. My old friend was unusually bright and breezy for the hour.

'What's your news then?' I asked a bit croakily. It was obvious she had some.

'Sita's coming home.'

'When?' I cleared my throat.

'Much earlier than expected. Today, in fact,' she said happily. 'Looks like I won't be around for a few days. Anyway, what happened last night? Two wine bottles, two glasses. You're not very good at hiding the evidence. Where is she? Under the bed?'

She made a play at pulling the mattress up.

'She went home,' I said, making for the bathroom.

'Before, after or during?'

'After, actually.'

'*Really?*' Julia hissed.

She hurried after me and sat on the toilet as I climbed into the shower. I couldn't think of a reason not to tell her, not that she would have left the house without some sort of reply.

'What a little hussy,' Julia said delightedly, after my short description. Nothing would have made her happier than for me to have some sort of tryst with somebody new. Even if it was Stephanie. 'And you're seeing her again?'

'I don't know. I don't think so.' I tried to explain. 'Maybe I'll ask her for lunch.'

'More shagging, less eating, if you want my advice,' Julia said, offering a crude option.

'Rein in that imagination, Julia,' I replied, soaping myself.

'My imagination is fine,' she retorted. 'Neither over-fertile nor under-nourished.' She paused. 'And how do you feel about all this?'

'How do you mean?' I yelled over the gushing water.

'She slept with you, she's married and, despite what she said, she's probably straight. How do you feel about *that*?'

'Julia, please. I don't want grilling.'

'I'm not the Gestapo,' she pointed out. 'I'm a concerned friend.' She said this without the slightest trace of humour.

'To be honest, I don't know how I feel,' I replied. 'I can't remember the last time I had an experience even close to this. It's really strange.'

'Do you still want her?'

'Julia! She's not a bag of chips.'

Her guffaw echoed around the bathroom. Eventually her unashamed and infectious laugh had me hooting along. When Julia set out to cheer somebody up, she rarely failed.

I stepped out of the shower and, shooing Julia from the bathroom, emerged a few moments later fully dried and sporting my new underwear.

'Ooh,' Julia said in approval. 'And who are we dressing to impress?'

It didn't take much effort to ignore her. She knew this was going nowhere and so asked me instead about Cynthia's letters.

'Well, for obvious reasons we didn't get a chance to look at them.'

Julia laughed. 'Where are they?'

Sighing, I retrieved them from the dresser and threw them across the bed. 'Come on, clever clogs, see what you make of them while I get dressed.'

Julia was poring over the letters when I went back into the bedroom in search of my shoes.

'My God,' she muttered. 'This Imrie really knows how to throw a spanner in the works, doesn't she?'

I smiled, remembering that's how I'd described Julia once upon a time. I took a seat next to her. The letters were scattered across the quilt.

'Let me read this to you. I'll translate. It's in Italian.

There has never been another lover quite like you. Of all the women I have known, and there have been others, as you know, no one has moved me as you do. Your smell, your taste, your hair and skin affect me, touch my soul beyond anything I've ever experienced. I don't know when I'll see you again, and if desire drives you into another's arms, think nothing of it. Do not hesitate if love or lust comes along, because I will always wait for you, I will always be here, and, if circumstances allow, I will be back in your arms one day.

'She's certainly got a way with words,' I said huskily, reminded of my own rekindled lust. 'Is that it?'

'Well, there's more in the same vein. All the letters in Italian are to do with sex. Well, sex and feelings. There are a couple in some European language I don't know...'

'Czech,' I explained.

'And the English letters are to do with, well, I'm not really sure. Hidden treasure, as far as I can make out, daft as it sounds.'

'Mmm. That's what Stephanie said.'

'I thought you'd been too busy for conversation.' Julia grinned.

'Not last night,' I said, poking her in the ribs.

'Your old Aunt Cynthia a dyke, eh? Calderton's best-kept secret.'

'A few more secrets than just that, I think.'

'There was one thing. Remember the business with your hand? Come on, let me look.'

I gave her my upturned palm as she shuffled through the letters.

'There,' she said, pushing a letter, one written in Czech, towards me. 'See? Written down, it looks more like a map.' She carefully examined my hand. 'They are almost the same, aren't they?'

I 'mmmd' noncommittally.

'It's a shame we can't get this translated. Not many Czechoslovakians in Calderton,' she muttered. 'You said your mother knows something, didn't you?' she went on.

'Yes, and if I knew where she was, I'm sure she'd tell me. If you get a minute, give her a ring. She'll drop anything to speak to you,' I said, retrieving my hand.

'Not quite anything,' Julia smirked.

'Julia! Do you mind? That's my mother you're talking about.'

'Got to go,' Julia said, stuffing the letters into some semblance of order. I've got clients to rob, taxes to fiddle.

Catch you later.' And with that she was down the stairs and off.

I toyed with looking at the letters myself, but Stephanie's note was somehow of more interest.

Letty,
I know you're not sure about all this and, to be honest, neither am I. I'll be at the Internet Café on Oxford Road at twelve. Meet me for coffee or a meal if you can. I really need to speak to you, and to see you again.
    Stephanie.

Excited and disturbed, I went to see to my livestock.

I didn't get to Manchester that day after all. Stephanie rang to chicken out of our meeting, date, whatever she chose to call it. Somehow her voice, over the phone, was different. She was quiet, almost subdued, not the woman of the previous evening.

'I'm sorry. I've got an appointment I'd forgotten about. Perhaps some other time?'

'Whatever.' I sighed, finding I was disappointed, despite what I'd said.

'No, really,' she insisted. 'I'll call you. Letty, is that okay?'

I thought for a minute. I supposed it would have to be okay. What else could I say?

'Stephanie, you've got my number. It's up to you.' I thought she would be satisfied with that.

'No, it's not,' she insisted quietly. 'It's up to us.'

'I don't know what you want from me,' I began.

'Yes, you do,' she said, almost whispering.

Her voice had a faded quality that quite took my breath away.

'We all make mistakes,' I said, trying to regain some control.

Suddenly she laughed. 'It was no mistake, Letty.'

I was stunned, her words were so surprising that, try as I might, I really couldn't think of a reply to that.

'Stephanie,' I began with some despair as a thousand emotions – well, maybe something a little more base than emotions – played havoc with my stomach. 'Stephanie, ring me, if you want to. We've still got things to discuss.'

'I know,' she said simply. 'I'll see you as soon as I can.' Our conversation ended on that note.

Chapter 27

The phone, the house, even the hens were strangely quiet on the run-up to Saturday. In the space of a few days, I was transported back to my pre-Anne life. And putting everything else aside for the moment, it gave me time to reflect on the inadequacies of the later stages of our relationship.

Loneliness, I discovered, was only marginally worse without her. Somehow the feeling gave me hope.

The jobs I'd done to fill the gaps now began to take on an importance of their own. I finished the bedroom, for one thing, with a rather gorgeous tin of apple-green paint I found lurking in the back of the garage. With each stroke of the brush, Anne's presence was diminishing.

It was a feeling, a scary feeling that, especially after my encounter with Stephanie, I was secretly beginning to enjoy. Music filled my house again, not just to stop the memories, or revive them either. The CD player got hammered simply for my own enjoyment. And being able to play my music as loud and as long as I wanted was suddenly, unexpectedly, liberating, though I could barely acknowledge this revelation. I had recovered enough to put the on/off dealings with Stephanie to the back of my mind and salvaged enough of my spirit to look forward to a night out at the pictures. I could even eat again too, and a meal in town suddenly appealed.

So, Saturday came around, as did my friends. Julia looked and acted like a twenty-five-year-old and Sita, professional, aloof and wise, indulged her partner.

Unannounced, they arrived in style in Sita's fancy car, accompanied by the threat of a storm. Clouds, heavy with rain and itching to dump their contents on the arid earth, gathered in the distance. The wind had picked up too, and the almost seaside smell that came along with the weather front seemed ominous. Sooner or later it was going to chuck it down.

'Letty, sweetheart,' Julia bellowed her arrival. 'Wow,' she said when she spied the house. 'Look at this.' The kitchen was polished to a degree that even AnnaMaria in her most aggravated state would have found acceptable.

'And look at you,' she chortled, taking in the sharp creases of my shirt and the tapered lines of my new pants. 'You look gorgeous. It's a shame it's too hot for velvet.' She took the fine cotton sleeve of my shirt between her fingers, testing the quality. 'Any news on the Stephanie front?' she whispered in an aside.

'Yes,' I said. 'But not now,' and I quickly ended the discussion.

Sita popped her head around the door. Those dark, arched eyebrows, perfectly plucked, almost austere, adorned black, mischievous eyes.

'Letty,' she said warmly. 'And how are you?'

She passed me a bunch of summer flowers, home-grown, their perfume heavy enough to cause havoc with sinuses more easily affected than mine. The pinks, phlox and lush, overblown, short-stemmed roses were interspersed with gypsophila, its delicate white flowers adding an uncultivated touch. Sita had an eye for such things.

Waving away my thanks, she kissed me gently, leaving the slightest, sweetest taste of lipstick on my mouth. She was a tall, regally built woman of indeterminate middle age. Solid and reliable, she oozed confidence and encouraged it in others. I knew Julia felt safe with her. So did I.

She was also quick to get a sense of things, of atmospheres, the ambience of a place. Still, the smell of paint, the almost showroom cleanliness of the farm and Abba's loud, 1970s camp, delivered a not-so-subtle message.

Sita didn't ask me about Anne. She didn't enquire after AnnaMaria or Liam. She did ask me, as Julia made a mess of flower-arranging, how the chickens were and how business was doing, and if I had been badly affected by the seemingly soon-to-be-over drought.

Apart from the local vet, nobody ever asked me about my livestock, and as virtually silent onlookers to my life, their position in the scheme of things was usually not so important. I could almost feel Julia raise an eyebrow as I blundered on about this safest of subjects. Eventually, my flowers duly subdued, she had to make a verbal protest.

'Before we go into the merits of Smith's Organic Hen Food, do you think we could start making tracks?' She stood pointedly between me and her lover.

Sita laughed, a cheerful explosive sound.

'Dinner's booked for half-six,' Julia explained. 'You can't just go wandering in when it suits, you know.'

Her lover sighed, indulgent again.

We squeezed into the Saab as the first of the thunder rolled in the distance. The hens clucked unhappily in their coop. Despite their distinct lack of imagination, the approaching storm jolted some primeval fear that years of domestication could not overcome. But they were safe enough where they were, whatever the weather.

The city was hot and clammy when we arrived, and it was a relief to get out of the car. Julia parked in the underground car park adjacent to Canal Street, in the heart of the gay village.

Not so surprisingly, knowing Julia, my friend and I had had some very strange experiences over the years. I'd suffered tiffs, terror and near-death due, in part, to her ability to get involved with things she really shouldn't mess with. She was almost as dangerous to know as Angela Lansbury. But dinner didn't hold any horrors. Velveteen was a very swish yet surprisingly inexpensive eatery and indigestion due to overeating proved to be the only problem I encountered.

A short journey to Belle Vue cinema showcase followed.

'What,' I demanded, unbuttoning my trousers with some relief, 'are we going to see?'

'A classic,' Julia said with a grin.

'Not subtitled?' I groaned. Sita barked a laugh.

'It doesn't have to be unless you have difficulty following early American.' Julia laughed too. 'Now, I know you've never seen this. In fact, you're probably the only person in the universe not to have viewed it at least once, so keep an open mind. Okay?'

'Okay,' I agreed.

Minutes later I was viewing the headlining films on offer. Trash filled cinemas one through to six and Julia's choice stood out clearly: *Gone With the Wind*.

'An epic that has stood the test of time', the advertising read. And who was I to argue?

Four hours or more of gorgeous colours and costumes, and hammy acting that was bafflingly appealing. There was a short break halfway through the film, time enough for the patrons to use the toilet, buy another bucket of popcorn or lavish the last of their change on ice cream.

At the queue to the third of these options a familiar voice, a *loud* and familiar voice had me craning over the shoulders of the middle-aged couple in front of me. Mrs Buckham's grey head and cardiganed shoulders blocked the entrance to the booth.

'What do you mean you haven't got chocolate?' and she turned to tut at her companion.

'Have an ice lolly,' Florence suggested. 'The strawberry ones are nice.'

The two women debated as the queue lengthened. A choice was finally made and they squeezed their way out.

'Sylvia,' I said as she edged towards me. 'Hiya.'

'Letty!' she squealed. 'How lovely to see you. How are you? How are *things*?' she added with a whisper.

'Not so bad.' I smiled. 'Hello, Florence. Is it *Gone With the Wind* then?'

'What else?' Florence sniffed. 'Have you seen the rubbish that's on? Millions, these films cost, and who's going to remember them in fifty minutes, never mind fifty years?'

I grinned as she tucked her arm into Sylvia's.

'Mind you, Jack's gone to see some double-bill horror thing, but he's only young yet. He'll learn,' Sylvia decided. 'Who are you here with?'

I explained my trip out with Julia.

'If you want, we'll drop you home. It'll save her a long journey,' the shopkeeper offered.

I thought a moment and nodded my agreement. I knew Julia wanted a night with Sita. We arranged to meet at the exit after the show.

Jack's Escort was basic but comfortable, and though it took a few minutes for Florence to ensure we were all safely strapped in, we were soon heading home, having left Sita and a grateful Julia to their night of passion.

There was nothing of the boy racer about Florence's grandson. Generally he kept his silence and observed the speed limit – unlike my other companions, who talked non-stop and at full pelt. At some point a small bottle of brandy was produced from Florence's cavernous handbag and the three of us non-drivers shared the contents. 'Now then,' Mrs Buckham began. 'We've still not had our chat.'

'Which one?' I asked.

She thought for a minute and took a swig of brandy. She breathed out loudly as the alcohol hit the back of her throat. 'Stephanie,' she hissed. 'And those letters.'

'Must we?' I asked.

'Secret letters in different languages? Palm-readings and all that? I should think so! And then there's that man she married,' she retorted, repeating herself to make sure I'd got the message. She chugged more brandy.

'What do you know about him?' I was intrigued in spite of myself.

'Land developer, by trade, or so he claims. And years older than his wife,' Florence interrupted, and she produced and lit a cigarette, waiting for my comment.

I wriggled with discomfort. If these two women had any idea about the involvement I'd had with his wife . . .

'Can't wait to get their hands on George's land,' Florence said loudly. 'Do them no good, though. Greed, that's all it is.'

'Do you still think it's something to do with the water?' Mrs Buckham asked innocently.

'Maybe, maybe not,' Florence replied evasively. She fiddled with her cigarette.

'I do like a mystery,' Mrs Buckham confessed suddenly. As if we didn't know.

'Brandy? Florence asked.

I took the bottle. There was a moment while my stomach debated sharing its already overcrowded contents. It decided there was room enough for a drop more of the strong stuff.

'I'm hoping to see my mum soon,' I explained to the two women. 'If I ever find out anything definite about those letters, don't worry, you'll be the first to know.'

'What languages were they written in?' Florence suddenly asked, eyes carefully holding mine.

'English mostly, and Italian, some of them. Julia translated those for me. Love letters they were.' I waited for a shocked comment, or at least some comment, but Florence said only, 'Oh?'

'And Czech. I didn't realise my aunt could speak it. Or Italian, come to that.'

'Well, there was always more to Cynthia than met the eye,' Sylvia offered, reinventing memories of my aunt. 'And she was as bad as your mother for holidays. Always swanning off somewhere or other. And she never once sent me a card, you know.'

I glanced at Sylvia as she wandered off into her own little world.

Florence looked thoughtful. 'Could I have a look at them? The ones you don't understand. I've got a friend from that part of the world. 'Course, she lives in Grimsby now.'

I waited.

'Came to England during the war,' she explained after another fortifying slug of brandy. 'You can let me have them when we drop you off.'

I nodded. At the time there seemed no reason not to.

Chapter 28

Jack dropped me off at the farm and I took a short cut up the porch to my bedroom to collect the letters. Jack declined offers of a coffee, wanting to prolong the evening about as much as I did. Disturbing his sleeping gran and her new friend would have been too much effort and he quietly wished me a polite 'Good night' before driving off.

I crunched down the dry gravel path. The storm still lurked overhead, the clouds' watery contents weighing heavily in the atmosphere. I could almost taste the electricity in the air and the heat and humidity oppressed me, each step feeling like ten. In seconds my clothes were soaking and sweat stung my eyes.

Passing the henhouse, I was rewarded with signs of life: a soft cluck from within and a quiet shuffle of dusty feathers.

Taking a moment to get my breath, I glanced into the coop. Water ran, a constant trickle from the yard's stoptap to keep the bowls constantly topped up and fresh. Any overflow was channelled into my vegetable patch, keeping at least the greens alive in the overbearing weather. I was particularly proud of this innovation and AnnaMaria had been pleased with my efforts at conservation. God, I'd be stuffing quilts with chicken feathers next.

Rounding the corner of my house towards the kitchen door, I almost walked into the back of my mum's BMW. Despite a build-up of steam, I could see her shadowy figure through the kitchen window. Quietly, I let myself in. She had her back to me and I had a few seconds, a few relieved seconds, to watch her as she pottered about.

We were inclined towards the same haircut and our features were similar enough to confirm the blood ties. Seaside fish and chips hadn't affected her waistline and whatever else Blackpool had to offer hadn't touched her figure either. If anything, she seemed thinner. Looking elegant and comfortable in shades of summer whites, her open-necked shirt, the collarless type, was long and crease-free (it's odd how you notice these things with my mother). Her trousers, in a creamy cotton, were three-quarter-length, revealing tanned feet comfortably encased in a pair of Clark's silver strappy sandals.

The radio was tuned into Easy Listening FM and she was humming along to a Matt Monro classic. Long-since dead, his mellifluous voice could still set her knees a-trembling. Though a little distracted, Margaret Campbell looked happy enough.

'Mum?' I ventured over Matt's tale of freed lions.

She looked up quickly, the tune dying on her lips, and she smiled. For once she didn't bite my head off for not using her forename.

'Good night?' she asked carefully.

'Entertaining, if you're into Scarlett O'Hara.' I laughed, still hovering by the back door.

'Tea?' she asked, temptingly waving a cup in my direction.

I burst into tears, which surprised us both. Suddenly maternal, Mum abandoned the brew and came over to me.

I caught the smell of jasmine on her skin and a darker hint of honey in her hair before I buried my face in the soft folds of her blouse.

'I'm so sorry about what's happened,' she whispered into my ear. 'I know how fond you were of Anne.'

I let her hold me for maybe half a minute, a long time considering our rather precarious relationship, before I pulled away, gripping her arms just above the elbows.

'Never mind Anne,' I croaked. 'Where have you been?'

She wasn't expecting this. And they weren't words I'd planned either. Her blank look of surprise melted into obvious distress.

'I've been so *worried*,' I went on.

'Letitia,' she said, shaking me off, 'you know where I've been. Do you know how worried I've been about you? I've had just one call, and that from AnnaMaria, explaining what had happened and more or less asking me to stay away.'

This was ridiculous. We led totally separate lives. I never expected her to explain her comings and goings. Why did this particular outing bother me?

'Well, you know how we argue,' I snapped. 'For Christ's sake, I felt bad enough.' I paused, realising with a jolt that we'd immediately fallen into our old pattern.

There was silence for the longest time.

'I'm sorry,' we said simultaneously. Mum smiled and I grinned guiltily. She put her arms around me and I didn't object as she patted my back and muttered the sympathetic things that mothers mutter in times of crisis.

'Tea?' she asked again, eventually releasing me.

The air, somehow, was cleared, at least for the time being, and she took a seat opposite me, two steaming cups between us. Suddenly we had nothing to say to each other, having found ourselves playing roles that neither of us had had much training for.

Mum reached for her handbag as the silence, broken

now by the Beatles playing 'Eleanor Rigby' (a song surely designed for such moments) stretched. She produced a tiny pack of tissues and a make-up case. Peering into a small, round, slightly smeared mirror, she repaired the physical damage that emotion had caused. Lipgloss, a dusting of face powder and a subtle shade of grey dabbed gently onto her eyelids and my mum could face the world again.

She smiled weakly at me. The stage was mine and I really had no idea how to begin.

'Perhaps I should start?' Mum suggested as I sought the right words. Heartbreak was not so easily explained.

'No, it's okay.' And in a roundabout way, in words that were difficult to choose and even more difficult to speak, I told her the short and brutal version of Anne's leaving.

Mum shed a few more tears herself, washing away the make-up she'd just repaired, and meanwhile we drank enough tea to clear China's national debt.

'Oh, Mum, let's talk about something else,' I said eventually. 'I can't bear this misery any longer.' I blew my nose. 'Come on, what's your tale then?'

She looked away. 'To be honest, I don't think this will cheer you up much, though it might explain a few things.'

She reached for her handbag, eventually pulling out the same letters I'd had lurking under the bed. But they weren't quite the same. These were originals, the paper crisp with age. Mum handled them gently.

'I first saw these,' she began, 'almost thirty years ago. Even then I knew how important they were.'

She rubbed her face tiredly and I noticed with a start how fine the skin on the backs of her hands had become. Veins stood out and tiny bones moved alongside the delicate muscles; muscles, bones and skin well past the height of their strength. She looked older and my heart, selfless for once, stirred for her.

'Look,' she said, recovering a bit. 'I'll tell you some of what I know, or rather what my sister told me. I never thought – ' She faltered for just a second. 'I never thought I'd be here telling you all this, and certainly not thirty years down the line. Cynthia told me her story from almost this exact same spot. The kitchen didn't look much different then either. The same pine walls, pine furniture too. But not this Ikea stuff that you are so fond of,' she said, laughing gently. 'It was 1968, and I still don't know what compelled her to tell me.' She ground to a halt until I waved for her to go on. 'Well, she swore she would burn them and I wonder, now, what stopped her. And to leave copies with her neighbour! It seems a pointless risk, though he kept them safe enough,' she added sadly. 'But I don't suppose George Evershaw could plan for his death, could he?'

Actually my neighbour had planned for his death, down to the last detail too, though even he couldn't have known when his last day was going to be.

'My God, how the past can torment you,' Mum whispered.

Torment seemed a strong word to use, but her thoughts were far away, so I didn't question her uncharacteristic choice.

'Okay,' I agreed quietly. 'Tell me Cynthia's story then.'

Mum spread the letters across the table in much the same way Stephanie had done a couple of weeks before.

'Cynthia was somewhat older than me, and the world was a lot different. Europe was a terrifying place in those days. The war had displaced so many people, destroyed so many lives. Our family was no exception. Of course, Cynthia wasn't caught up in it in quite the same way as, say, our brother, but she worked hard then. She was in the Land Army. A Land Girl,' she added quietly and smiled. 'Do you know, there was always speculation as to why she never had relationships of her own. After Imrie there was no one. I'm sorry, I'm getting ahead of myself.' Mum paused and checked her watch. For a second I didn't think she was going to go on. Doubt floated through her eyes, but finally she put her reservations aside. The story she told me left me speechless.

Chapter 29

Well-kept family secrets are rarely revealed as dramatically. From a slightly mysterious older figure, Cynthia was suddenly propelled into the sort of character I thought existed only in John Le Carré's imagination.

I stared at my mother.

'It's true, you know,' she said defensively. 'Whatever Cynthia was, she wasn't a liar.'

I squirmed uncomfortably. 'But why? Why would she get involved in something like this?'

Mum thought a minute. 'She was in love. Isn't that why we do a lot of things? And because she loved her brother too. They were always close, you know, much closer than he was to me.'

'But you still see him every year. Well, except this year,' I pointed out.

Suddenly Mum laughed. 'I couldn't this year. He's got a new man in his life.'

'Uncle George? He's eighty if he's a day!' I exclaimed.

'Don't knock it,' she said smiling wistfully. 'I'm going to have to tell him about the letters, though. It's going to stir up an awful lot of trouble.'

Trouble? That wasn't the half of it.

Once Mum had got into her stride, her story, told in fits and starts, had left me open-mouthed and doubtful of the Campbell family's sanity.

Imrie, Cynthia's lover, had been shipped over from Europe just before the war began. A teenager, part Jewish, part Gypsy, she was vulnerable to the terror that had begun to grip the world. Her family had enough money for a single one-way trip, and managed to smuggle her to England and the safety of Calderton to work as a Land Girl with Cynthia on the farm. Cynthia never explained how she'd come to be in this unusual position, though Mum managed to throw some light on it.

'Your Uncle George was a naval officer, based at the British Embassy in Prague, and somehow, I don't know how, he'd got involved with Imrie's family. For whatever reason, he helped Imrie get to England. It was just as well really. Only her mother survived the war.'

'But the other stuff, the smuggling, the art works, the paintings she was on about, how – '

Mum waved me to silence. 'Imrie's mother became involved with the underground movement in Prague when the German's invaded in 1938. Her husband was a curator of Prague's Kinsky Museum. You've probably never heard of it.'

I shook my head.

'You must look it up sometime. He was still curator for a while under occupation. It was pretty obvious to them that the works held at the museum wouldn't be there for long. A couple of Renoirs had already been taken to Germany, the rest of the collection would disappear before long too. You have to understand just how important the works were to these people, especially in financial terms. I know we've argued about things like this before.'

She smiled at me. Argued? We'd been like cat and dog on the merits or otherwise of the worth of such 'treasures'. When Van Gogh's 'Sunflowers' had sold for God knows how much to a Japanese collector, I'd had a rant about the cost of such an item that to me, was still only a bit of old paint on a canvas. Especially as the poor sod who painted it had died mad and penniless. Mum (no surprise there) had taken the opposite view.

'Anyway, from what I've learned since, it's obvious that the paintings and some of the more valuable sculptures were whisked away before they could be taken to Germany. It's hardly anything new. Even the galleries in England were emptied, supposedly to protect them from bombing,' Mum continued.

'Did you meet this Imrie?' I asked.

'Probably, but I don't really remember to be honest. I wasn't even at school then. My brother used to visit when he was on leave, I do remember that.'

'So,' I said, trying to get a clearer picture. 'He was the middle man in all of this. It was my Uncle George who smuggled the stuff from the museum?'

'I suppose that's the simplistic way of looking at it,' she said. The sarcasm wasn't deliberate, I knew my mother well enough to realise that. 'Though there were others involved, including his commanding officer.'

'Who was?' I asked, suddenly getting an inkling of where this was going.

'Sir Claude Adam,' she said patiently. She put her hand up to stop any stunned questions. 'Apparently he was the guiding force behind it all.' She paused and looked away. 'They managed to keep going for months. It was only when war finally broke out and the Embassy staff were forced to flee that the deception was uncovered. I don't suppose I need to tell you what happened to most of the people involved.' She paused and looked down at her hands. 'Anyway, Cynthia explained that the fakes had been put in place when each original piece was transported abroad. Artists had copied and replaced every item earmarked for safe-keeping.'

Apparently the undertaking had involved the Prague underground, members of the Czech government, my uncle and Sir Claude, his boss.

And Cynthia. Cynthia, Yorkshire chicken farmer and receiver of stolen goods.

'So what did she do with them?'

'She hid them.'

'I know, but where? And why? Couldn't she have turned them over to someone?'

Mum fumbled with her cup and poured more tea.

'She'd made a promise. Both to Imrie and to Sir Claude, whom she trusted at that point. He was her brother's superior officer, why shouldn't she? Anyway, until Imrie came back to her, she swore she'd never let them out of her sight. But Imrie never came back. She went to America for reasons I can only guess at. There were plenty of Nazis lurking about and she'd had some anonymous threats. Her letters make it clear that she felt unsafe. Perhaps she thought relatives had escaped there. I don't know. We do know she went back to Prague when her mother was ill. I've no idea what happened to her after that. I assumed she was dead.'

'And Cynthia died still clinging to the secret.'

Mum smiled at the melodrama and nodded.

'I searched the farm of course, and all the surrounding land, but I found nothing. I couldn't convince her to reveal exactly what she'd hidden, or where she'd hidden it.' She sighed.

'And my uncle? Surely you talked about it?' It sounded like a stupid question, but considering the lack of communication so far perhaps it was not so ridiculous.

She looked away. 'Oddly enough, no. I tried on many occasions but he refused to discuss it.' She paused. 'I think when Sir Claude died, he assumed Cynthia would finally hand the art back to the appropriate authorities.'

I'd met my Uncle George a few times and what I remembered of him didn't quite fit into this strange picture. He was a gay man, living an elderly gay man's life in San Franisco's Bay area. I couldn't see him any other way.

'But she didn't. Why?'

'I told you, she made a promise to Imrie. Almost a pact really, that she would hold onto them until Imrie came back. She refused to believe that Imrie was dead. Of course, your Uncle George was livid. This went completely against the grain. He was basically an honourable man and, according to Cynthia, he felt the time had come to put everything right. To clear his conscience, so to speak. Cynthia never even told him where she'd hidden everything. It was the one thing that caused a rift between them.'

'He could have gone to the authorities, though, couldn't he?'

Mum looked troubled. 'No, not your Uncle George, not against his own family. Despite everything, that wasn't his way at all.'

'One other thing,' I said, when I realised she wasn't going to go on. 'How come George Evershaw had copies of Cynthia's letters? Why would she leave them with him?'

Mum shrugged, having no answer.

'And Stephanie came across them by accident, you think? She didn't seem any wiser than me.'

'Who knows?' she replied. 'Are you likely to see her again?'

A loaded question, I knew. I shifted in my seat, suddenly embarrassed.

'Her uncle's will-reading is on Monday, in Manchester. She'll be there.'

Mum got up to put the kettle on.

I shuffled through the letters scattered across the pine table. Those in Italian, it was even more evident now, were intimate correspondence. When Julia had translated them, the two women's love of the language, and their love for each other, had come over loud and clear.

Mum took her seat again. 'Look, I know how ridiculous this all sounds But frankly I don't give a damn *what* it sounds like.'

Rarely one to use post-watershed language, her outburst was a shock. It's strange, the power of speech. Julia could eff and blind with the best of them and I would barely notice. Mum chooses to say 'damn' and I nearly fall off my chair.

'I never wanted to believe any of this . . .' She foundered for a moment. 'You've no idea how it affected my relationship with Cynthia. I tried to persuade her just to hand it all back.' She suddenly broke off and got up to wander nervously around the kitchen. 'But she wouldn't. Remember, it was 1968. Just the time when the Czech people were going through another political upheaval.' She sighed. 'If a letter hadn't turned up, I would never have told you.' She held my gaze in hers, challenging me to make something of that statement. She didn't realise that if the situation had been reversed, I wouldn't have told her either.

She took a calming breath. 'What the letters didn't explain or at best only alluded to, well, you'll have to take the rest of what I said on trust.'

I had problems believing my aunt's outrageous tale. But who could I ring to check it out? MI5? The FBI?

'What about this then?' I asked, holding my palm towards her.

She took my hand in hers and smiled. 'Did you know you've got Cynthia's eyes too? She always had a mind for things like this, though, so I wouldn't set too much store by it if I were you. When Gypsies were in the area, she always went to them to get her palm read. You've no idea how many pegs I found when I cleared the farm out after she died.'

I smiled. 'Look, a lot of this still isn't very clear. I mean I don't understand why your brother didn't just tell his superiors? Never mind all this blood thicker than water crap.'

She turned to me. 'You don't understand, do you?' Frustrated, she ran a hand through her hair. 'George's immediate superior was the *only* person he reported to. Remember just how shadowy the whole venture was. And his commanding officer chose to keep the whole thing quiet.'

I looked at her in surprise. 'So,' I said, 'his boss never said anything then?'

'No,' she said abruptly. She looked me in the eye. 'Isn't it obvious that his reasons for keeping quiet were a lot less honourable than my brother's?'

Chapter 30

By the time she'd gone to bed it was almost dawn. I didn't bother following her upstairs. Sleep, for me, was an impossible dream. Instead, I went outside. Beating the cockerels to their early morning reverie, I let them out of their coop. Following my mood, their crowing and feeding were half-hearted affairs.

Familiar views were obscured by mist gathering across the fields. It felt eerie and the landscape was almost unreal. I shuffled down my yard to lean on the fence dividing George's farm from mine. It had looked dilapidated before but now it seemed as though a good storm and downpour would finally bring the old building to its foundations. The walls were beginning to lean dangerously and the roof tiles, particularly on the farmhouse, were being shed on an almost daily basis.

An odd sort of regret filled me and for a moment I wanted to flee from here. If I could believe what I'd learned, and I was desperately trying to make sense of it all, then the mysteries of the place were overwhelming. My former sense of peace was being eroded rapidly.

Of course, losing Anne had made things a hundred times worse than they would have been, and with her insight and support I could have coped. I sighed. Anne would never support me again and, though the worst of that particular heartbreak (I hoped) was over, the years did seem to stretch ahead.

A car heading down the path suddenly lifted my spirits. Squinting against a rapidly rising sun, I spotted a familiar figure in the front seat of a taxi. The Toyota bounced over the solid track and AnnaMaria's grin shone through the windscreen. A rich mixture of relief and happiness flooded me and I waved at her furiously. The car screeched to a halt near the coop and chickens flapped and squawked at its arrival.

Liam was in his push chair and AnnaMaria was suddenly in my face. Flinging her arms around my neck, she crushed the breath from my lungs.

'I've missed you,' she roared. 'What's been happening? How have you been keeping? What's the news? Why is your mum here? I saw the car. Is Julia still around?'

'Hang on, hang on,' I said, freeing myself from her embrace. 'I wasn't expecting you today.'

'Please!' she said. 'You can't keep me away from a good will-reading.'

'You've not forgotten then?'

'Calderton's summer highlight? I don't think so! Anyway, Julia rang to remind me, and I missed you and I'm skint, so there are three good reasons for coming back.'

Browner than ever, she looked even healthier than she had before.

'Come on, you lovely thing, let's make you some breakfast.'

We retrieved a still-sleeping Liam and trundled into the farm. Somehow I had to tell her all that had happened since her departure, all the strange things that I'd learned, but first I wanted to hear her news. Anything I had to say could wait.

'Then Mrs Rossi took us all to the country. I had no idea the outskirts of such a big city could be so beautiful. One minute we were smack in the bustle of Milan and ten minutes later we were in scenery gorgeous enough to knock your eyes out. I've got some photos developed. I'll dig them out later. Anyway, for God's sake, shut me up. I've already done the cabbie's head in.' She laughed and attacked the remains of her breakfast. 'What's been happening here then?' she asked between mouthfuls of toast.

It wasn't easy to tell her and I wasn't sure if I should. I was also loath to wipe the smile from her face. But, bless her, it only changed her expression from one of cheerfulness to one of amazement. Fortunately my story didn't affect her appetite and she munched thoughtfully as I brought her up to date.

'Bloody hell,' she said when I'd finished, her eyes on stalks. 'I can't leave you for five minutes.'

Put so succinctly, the news suddenly didn't weigh so heavily.

'You know what we've got to do now, don't you?' she asked, pushing her plate to one side.

I hardly dared ask. 'What?'

'Start digging,' she said with a grin.

I laughed into my tea. 'And what do you expect to find? I've not exactly been tripping over Renoirs for the last ten years.'

'More's the pity.' AnnaMaria smirked.

'And where would you suggest we start?' I asked, indicating the size of the area with a vague wave of my hand. 'Let's face it, we've no real idea of what we're looking for.'

'So let's just look for something then. Let me have another rummage through those letters of Cynthia's. And I could do with some exercise. Flying is all very well, but my backside went dead after the first hour. So, we'll start – ' She thought for a minute. 'In the garage. Then there's the barn. What about your cellar? You never go down there. Failing all that, we'll have a mooch through George's farm. Perhaps we should do that first. It looks as though it'll fall down any minute. And if Stephanie gets her mitts on it tomorrow, it might be the only chance we get. God, let's get cracking. I can't wait to find something.' She was unstoppable.

'So you believe it all then?' I ventured. 'Don't you think it all sounds a bit, well, over the top?'

'Actually, no,' she said. 'I'd believe anything of your family. I bet there's more rumours about Cynthia than anyone else in the village. Including George. Trouble is, you don't get involved enough in their gossip!'

She glanced over at Liam. Still in his push chair, he showed no signs of waking up.

My eyes were becoming gritty and sore, lack of sleep and too much excitement taking its toll. 'Look, I've got to go to bed. The digging will have to wait. What about you? Aren't you tired after your journey?'

'Nah, I slept most of yesterday. I'm sorry I didn't ring. I wanted to ask you how you were getting on without... you know.'

'Don't worry. I'm learning to cope. I've got more than enough to keep my mind occupied.'

'Anything new on George yet?'

'Not a peep. The coroner's report still hasn't been made public. I don't know what the hell they're waiting for. The neighbours are a nervous enough lot as it is. Anyway,' I said, squeezing her cheek, 'I'm so glad to see the pair of you again, but I'm afraid I'm going to have to catch some sleep. Wake me at dinner time, will you?'

She leaned across the table and kissed my forehead. 'Get to bed before you collapse.'

Chapter 31

AnnaMaria didn't wake me until two, by which time Mum had gone home. Sunday lunch beckoned. Vegetable pie and salad wouldn't suit; lamb roast with all the trimmings was more her style. Especially as, according to AnnaMaria, she'd been invited to lunch by her boss. I could picture the scene. Sitting around his huge oak dining table with a glass-eyed Bambi peering from one wall and ancient Italian artefacts on the other. My mother felt she had definitely been born into the wrong class. Probably the wrong era too.

She left me a 'don't worry too much' and 'we'll talk again soon' type of note and a mobile phone (she had two for some reason) in case I needed to reach her in a hurry.

Liam hadn't forgotten me in our weeks apart and he crawled over my bed in his enthusiasm to greet me.

'I had a word with your mum, though she wasn't thrilled that you told me,' AnnaMaria said. 'But she filled me in on a few more details. Stuff I could have done without, to be honest. I thought your mum was one on her own, but Cynthia! It must run in the family. God almighty!' She sighed, shaking her head in amazement. 'Anyway, I rang Andy. He said he'd come and look after Liam for the day, perhaps take him to a local football match. You'll love that, won't you?' she said to Liam ruffling his hair.

He giggled his reply.

'You've not changed your mind then?'

'As if!' She ran a hand through her own hair. Having abandoned the Björk-type bumps, her hair sat in a neat expensive crop around her face – Mrs Rossi's gentle persuasion, at a guess.

'Come on,' she ordered. 'Let's get cracking.'

Andy arrived twenty minutes later, adoration for Liam and his ex-partner shining in his eyes. Tall and gangly, he had to look down a considerable distance to peer at me and even then he rarely spoke more than a few words.

Clutching a football, he took his small charge around to the ancient minivan he managed to keep running and they set off for the local football ground.

AnnaMaria led me to the porch. The air was thick and hotter than ever. A heat haze hovered at ground level.

'Not rained then?' she observed.

'It's been threatening, but no sign of it yet.'

'Weird weather,' she muttered.

'Weird weather, weirder situation,' I commented.

AnnaMaria insisted on searching my garage first, but as the tidiest, most-used outbuilding on the farm it was no great surprise when we turned up nothing. By this time I'd almost forgotten the whole point of the exercise. My inclination to believe everything I'd been told about Cynthia had only a brief life-span and by the time we'd scoured the garage, unearthing only the odd dead mouse, my natural cynicism was firmly back in place.

'I should ring the doctor, you know,' I said loudly.

'Oh?' AnnaMaria asked, rubbing damp and dusty

171

hands down the front of her jeans. 'Who for?'

'My mother.'

'Worried about her mental state, are you?'

The fact that she'd read my thoughts was no surprise. Years spent living together had linked first our menstrual cycles and now our minds.

'I shouldn't be, if I were you,' she said.

'AnnaMaria, what are you driving at? What else did she say to you?'

'It's not so much what she said as the way she said it.' She paused, thoughtful. 'You know Sir Claude, Stephanie's step dad?' She leaned against my parked Land Rover and went on. 'Well, I rang Janice from the *Echo* first thing this morning. Asked her to get me a copy of the will. It's surprising what she can get at such short notice.'

'You rang Janice? And she wasn't curious?'

'Oh, it nearly killed her. You know I can't stand her, but she was happy to co-operate when I promised to explain later.'

'And his will? Why?'

'A hunch, that's all,' she said evasively.

A hunch? Mmm.

'Come on. I'll check the fax. Maybe something's come through.'

We trudged out of the dimly lit garage into shimmering sunshine beyond. Hens lolled lazily in the heat and as we crossed the yard and headed towards the house, the fax's clicking and beeping could be heard. My home's only remaining concession to high-tech (Anne had removed everything else) was about to reveal information I couldn't ignore.

Chapter 32

'My God, there's reams of the stuff,' AnnaMaria yelled from the hallway. 'It only costs two quid to get a copy, you know.' That fact would sit in the department of my brain marked 'Useless Information' for the rest of my days.

'Make a brew,' she demanded. 'It's going to take ages to plough through this lot. Sir Claude must have been worth a fortune,' she added as she brought the curly faxed pages into the kitchen.

The will had been drafted more than thirty years ago and though not knowing how such things were worded nowadays, I found the whole thing long-winded, almost quaint.

'My God,' she said quietly, her cup halfway to her mouth.

'What?' I asked, startled.

'You'll never guess who Sir Claude's solicitor was.'

But, after a thoughtful moment, I could.

'Richardson and Smedley, eh? My, how the plot thickens,' I muttered. 'I knew they'd been around a while.'

'Well, you know how these firms are passed on. *From generation unto generation.*'

'Coincidence, do you think?'

Her questioning look said it all.

We read the will between us, passing pages back and forth in case we missed anything.

'Here we go,' AnnaMaria said excitedly a few minutes later. 'Just as I thought. Listen to this: "I hereby bequeath and so on and so forth",' she mumbled half to herself and then added loudly, '"Calderton Brook Farm to my sitting tenant", who just happened to be your Aunt Cynthia.' She threw the page at me and grinned.

'Hang on,' I said as I read the script. 'What did you mean "Just as I thought"?'

'Nothing,' she said innocently. She drank tea, her bright eyes watching me over the cup's edge. 'I'm just a genius,' she said eventually.

'Why did he leave the farm to Cynthia anyway, and not his son?'

AnnaMaria sighed. 'Sir Claude and his son were estranged, remember? Perhaps Sir Claude blamed him for his first wife's death. He probably knew Cynthia wouldn't do anything with the art. And there was a bit more at stake than just a farm. He was a well-known figure. An untarnished reputation and a place in the history books mean a lot to someone like that. It would be nice to think he left the farm to Cynthia out of guilt, but somehow I doubt it.'

'But surely Cynthia could have told someone by then. The government, the press, handed it back to that Czech museum, whatever?' I groped for a more acceptable solution.

'Yes, but your mum said she promised to keep it to herself until Imrie came back. And hand it back? Remember the year? The stuff had already been snatched from under Hitler's nose. I can't imagine she'd want to hand it to the Russians on a plate.'

Next to metalwork, modern history had been AnnaMaria's favourite school subject.

'The whole thing is too bloody weird,' I said.

'Weird enough to believe?' AnnaMaria queried, a curious look on her face.

Definitely weird – but nothing compared to what happened next.

Chapter 33

I awoke the following day to the sound of rain. It was the sort of Monday morning downpour that every office worker in the land dreads getting up to.

This particular farmer wasn't keen on it either.

AnnaMaria was up, out and gone, along with her son and, I suspected, Andy. I wondered if she'd rekindled that particular flame, but she played most things so close to her chest, I knew there would be no point in asking her outright. She'd left me a note, though, a magnet holding it fast to the fridge.

We've got the thing in Manchester at four. Pick me up at the garage. Sorry, I haven't got time to search the premises today! Andy needs me here. See you later, AM xxx.

Staring out of the window, I realised that the weather put the mockers on any digging I may have decided to do myself. So compared to what I'd had to put up with lately, I had a normal enough morning. Too mundane to report here.

I spent an hour getting ready for an afternoon at my neighbour's solicitors. Stephanie's face kept getting in the way and, despite everything, my crush was alive and well and living in the vicinity of my crotch. I was also plagued with distant memories of my aunt which brought on a sinking, plummeting sensation in the pit of my stomach. It was a curious combination of feelings.

Recent events kept rolling through my mind. My dreams had been full of violence and I'd woken up with a leaden feeling in my gut. All I wanted to do was pack a bag and bugger off abroad for three months. But I couldn't do that. Where would I go?

I sat on the edge of my bed and as I struggled into my shoes my eyes fell upon the metal chest I kept at the side of my bookcase. My old photos were still in there. I'd not been tempted to force the lock and gaze at six years of memories. Something prompted me now, though, but it wasn't Anne's pretty face or fading look of love. Somewhere at the bottom were old family photos as well. Mum on cycling holidays. Dad with various cars he'd owned over the years. And images of Cynthia too. Suddenly I needed to see her face.

It didn't take much effort to break into the box. A few seconds with a sturdy pair of scissors and I soon had it open. At the bottom, as I'd hoped, beneath holiday snaps, Liam at different stages of his development and Anne proudly holding her book, was a small bundle of creased black and white photos. I spread them across the bed to study them. Strangers peered back at me. Who were these people forever caught in the past?

Women in tailored Forties-style suits smiled uncertainly at the camera. Only Cynthia was familiar. She looked robust, even as a young woman. She was alone on all the pictures bar one. Another woman, dark-haired, pencil-slim and dressed in a close-fitting boiler suit, clung to Cynthia's arm. There was something oddly familiar about that tight smile.

Was this Imrie? I looked for clues in the background. Snow obscured everything. It could have been taken anywhere, I turned the photo over. The year 1942 was written in faded black ink in one corner and an illegible photographers stamp covered the other. I put it to one side. Maybe Mum could have a look at it.

The conversation on the trip to the city was, unsurprisingly, concerned with George's soon-to-be revealed will. We agreed that Stephanie was going to get the lot. Farm, contents and whatever else the land might expose. AnnaMaria was increasingly convinced that Cynthia's secret stash would be found on George Evershaw's land.

It was raining in Manchester too – nothing new there – and the streets were almost deserted. But it was well after lunchtime and the city's workers were busy beavering away in offices scattered across the metropolis.

Richardson and Smedley were situated smack in the middle of the banking area and their premises reflected the sort of client group they represented. Seven storeys of glass and concrete towered up from the pavement. Nestled between the Bank of China and a less than trendy Eighties-style bar, itself formerly a bank, it was an impressive sight, and a slightly daunting one too. The glass doors and floor-to-ceiling windows allowed an unobstructed view into the reception hall.

'Stop dawdling, Letty,' AnnaMaria commanded as I edged my way up the ramp to the minimalist front door, all shimmering glass without a knob in sight. 'You've got as much right to be here as anybody. After all, George did specifically want you here, didn't he?'

'He insisted that I should be at the reading,' I said.

'Without you, half the family wouldn't have turned up.'

'Considering the circumstances, that might not have

been a bad thing.'

'Rubbish!' she said. 'Come on.' And she pushed me through the doorway.

Clerks in neat black suits stalked past, briefcases and folders clutched in their oh-so-busy hands. A guard watched us go past and the receptionist himself kept a keen eye out as we made our way to his huge curved desk.

'Madam,' he said as we approached. 'How may I help?'

'We're here for the will-reading of George Norman Edward Evershaw,' I explained.

'Letty?' a voice said behind me. Stephanie was guarded as she approached me, though somehow I had the feeling she was pleased to see me. I got a blast of hormonally influenced infatuation again. And a vivid memory of her hair on my pillow.

'I'll take it from here,' she instructed the clerk behind the desk.

As AnnaMaria suppressed a giggle, I made breathless introductions.

'We're upstairs,' Stephanie said, and we silently followed her into a lift. I didn't know what to say. It was the perfect awkward moment.

'Is there a toilet?' AnnaMaria asked, almost giggling on the spot. We dropped her off at the third floor with instructions on how to get to the appropriate office when she'd finished. Stephanie and I continued our journey in silence until finally we arrived on the top floor.

The doors opened onto a large gardened area. Not quite what I'd expected. Indoor plants, healthy and green, were everywhere. Tall yuccas stood in ornamental pots and their smaller exotic cousins filled every available surface. Stephanie turned to me. Her distinctive perfume reminding me of our intimate moments together.

'I wanted to speak to you alone. Is that all right with you?' I nodded. It would be fine as long as she did all the talking.

'I've not been in touch and I'm sorry, but I meant to,' she rambled.

She took my arm and guided me to a soft dark-blue settee placed in front of a large window. The views of Manchester's wet concrete jungle were interrupted by a huge office block across the street. Crossing her legs, her tights made soft shushing noises against her short black skirt. She leaned towards me. If she tried to kiss me I would jump out of the window, I thought crazily. Instead she took my hand and ran her finger over the markings on my palm. I felt faint.

'Have you discovered anything about the letters?' she asked.

I was stunned by her question. I'd expected something a little more intimate than that. And suddenly, though I wasn't sure why, I felt rather used.

'No,' I lied quickly. 'They're still as big a mystery to me as they are to you,' though as I spoke I realised that wasn't true. She knew exactly what was behind them, I was almost positive of it.

Stephanie checked her watch. 'We'd better be getting on. Ruth will be ready to do the reading now.' She paused. 'About the other night, perhaps we could . . .' she began.

'I don't think so,' I muttered, trying hard not to sound regretful. 'Like I said, we all make mistakes.'

She sighed and smiled and ran the back of her fingers down my face. It took everything I had, but I managed to pull away. She took the brush-off with good grace, better than I would have managed, and we returned to the lift. Silent again, we went back to the third floor.

Ruth Smedley's office was huge and the room was dotted with familiar and not so familiar faces. Florence dozed in a low-backed Habitat-style settee and Mrs Buckham fidgeted beside her. She waved as I made my entrance. AnnaMaria was staring through the window and Claude, the man I'd never actually met, watched me, expressionless, from across the room. I stared back, taking in the good suit and silk shirt. He was much older than Stephanie and his grey hair, receding from an already wide forehead, was tied into a rocker's ponytail at the back. A peculiar mixture of styles; you'd notice him in a crowd.

Three or four more elderly people sat opposite Ruth's large, empty desk. George's relatives were a diverse bunch but they all smiled in recognition.

Jack hadn't made the reading – he'd probably had quite enough of Florence after the last outing.

One unusual figure towered by the doorway. A mass of brown curly hair floated around a head topped by a yarmulke with fancy designs which confirmed the Jewish origins of its wearer. Even white teeth glinted from behind an equally curly and rather magnificent beard.

Ruth Smedley stepped from beyond a recessed door partially hidden by more pot plants. She was another one in a classy black suit, but with that fair hair pinned up in a French pleat and an unspoken aura of leadership, it was clear she outranked the rest of the staff. A pair of modern and narrow-framed glasses added to the appearance of power. She didn't need that touch; the suit, the hair and the offices said it all.

'I'm sorry to have kept you waiting,' she said to the small gathering. 'And I do apologise for the delay in the reading. In the event of his death, Mr Evershaw had left personal instructions with me to contact Rabbi Burns here of the Jewish Liberal Peace Organisation of London and Tel Aviv.' She smiled. 'I'm afraid Rabbi Burns took some tracking down. Anyway, if you could all just take a seat, we can begin.' She acknowledged her audience but seemed to take a long moment to scrutinise me.

I wondered for a moment why George hadn't asked me to contact the Rabbi. And who was he? There was nothing Jewish about George. He was Chapel through and through.

The Rabbi grinned a greeting, his eyes holding AnnaMaria's for just a second. She smiled, slightly taken aback, and a flush crept across her cheeks. What was this? Lust at first sight?

We shuffled into position, though AnnaMaria remained where she was as I squashed up by the side of a sleepy Florence and a wide-awake Sylvia Buckham.

'Now, normally,' Ruth said, 'the will of the deceased is available for all those involved to examine at their leisure. However, under Mr Evershaw's instructions his bequests, drawn up privately by himself but kept in readiness in this office, are to be revealed only during this reading. To be honest, his final instructions are a mystery to me too.'

Curious that George should draw up his will himself and then pay this lot for the privilege of keeping it safe. I wondered who had witnessed it.

The document was short, sweet and devastating.

I hereby leave my van and all my work tools to my next-door neighbour, Letty Campbell.

I smiled to myself. The whole lot was worth about a fiver. Sweet thought though.

I hereby leave all my furnishings to Sylvia Buckham of Ye Olde Corner Shop, Calderton.

Another fiver. Probably even less than that after Stephanie's rummage through the place.

I hereby leave my watch to Jack Walker (Flo's grandson).

It was a Casio and as such wouldn't even make it to the fiver mark, though Jack was included in the sum of twelve thousand pounds that was to be split equally between his relatives.

That caused a few intakes of breath, mine included. Judging by George's lifestyle, I would have thought he'd be hard pressed to scrape together twelve pounds. I worked it out and I reckoned that gave Stephanie about fifteen hundred in cash to play with. His much-sought-after land wasn't quite the last to go.

I hereby leave the sum of one hundred and twenty thousand pounds to The Jewish Liberal Peace Organisation of Tel Aviv and London.

Stunned silence. Not Chapel then, after all.

Everything else, my farm, my freehold estate, outbuildings and all they contain, I hereby leave to...

I watched Stephanie, already shocked and openmouthed, and her husband out of the corner of my eye.

...my cousin Florence Shaw of Huddersfield, to do with as she sees fit.

Florence woke up as Mrs Buckham crashed an elbow into her ribs.

'What?' she asked loudly. Sylvia whispered the news into her ear.

'Oh,' she said, and smiled over at me, her long thin face breaking into wrinkled delight. She glanced across the room and her gaze fell on Rabbi Burns. An almost imperceptible nod passed between them. I don't think anyone noticed but me.

Even Ruth Smedley looked surprised, and Claude? If he could have willed Flo (not to mention the Rabbi) to drop dead at that moment, no one would have been happier.

The will was signed, witnessed, sealed and in correct legal order, as Ruth pointed out to an enraged Claude. He stormed out of the room, followed hurriedly by his wife. Stephanie gave me one lingering glance before she disappeared through the door.

'I think that calls for a celebration, don't you?' Florence

suggested through her smiles. 'I'm eighty-two,' she reminded me as she struggled to her feet. 'Do you think I'm too old to start farming?'

The trouble was, she was serious.

Ruth Smedley called her over to sign documents and collect the farm's legal ownership papers, and half an hour later we were back on the street, Florence, on paper at least, about a hundred and fifty thousand pounds richer.

'Where's AnnaMaria?' Mrs Buckham asked.

I craned my neck for a look into the reception area and I spotted her chatting to the hairy Jewish chap. Personal space was being invaded, though neither of them seemed to mind. He handed a card over and they shook hands, once, twice, a third time. Much laughing accompanied the act. AnnaMaria, it was clear to me, was smitten. I hoped for her sake he was based in London and not Tel Aviv.

Eventually she joined us. 'He's nice,' was all she would say. But for the rest of it, she was beyond delighted. 'Did you see Claude's face?' she cackled as we struggled through the rain-soaked, wind-blasted streets of Manchester.

'Well, I'm glad he didn't get it,' Sylvia said. 'To expect so much and then get nothing. Just greed, that's all it was. I told you, didn't I? Funny about the Rabbi, though. And George, my goodness! He usually had the morals of a slug,' she said, abandoning her previous, and false, stand over George's character. 'I wonder if he was Jewish? I wonder if the Methodist minister knows?' she added, clearly surprised at the outcome of the will.

I resisted a comment.

I had the older women on either arm. Flo was as insubstantial as candy floss, while Sylvia clung on, as tenacious as an ivy.

AnnaMaria danced ahead of us. 'Ring Julia and tell

her,' she urged. 'She'll love this. And your mum,' she added.

'It'll keep,' Florence insisted. She stopped in her tracks. 'This'll do,' she said and led us all into Bar 28, the classiest joint on this side of town.

Metal spiral staircases led apparently nowhere and the cheapest bottled beer was nearly three quid a throw, but Florence really didn't seem to care.

'I'll drive if you want a drink,' AnnaMaria offered generously. 'I can give us all a lift home then. Assuming you're coming home, Florence?'

'Try and stop me,' she chortled. 'Sylvia, throw those train tickets away. We're going home in style!'

Chapter 34

There was a point during the following hour when I felt I should tell my two companions about recent events. I knew Sylvia still wondered about the letters, though Florence, curiously enough, hadn't mentioned the ones in her possession. But AnnaMaria advised against it.

'Look,' she said, as the two women toddled off to the loo, 'let it lie. If there is anything there, Florence will or won't find it, and whatever connections Claude had to the property have been severed now. He can't get his hands on the place. My God, and all that money George left! I think he probably had the last laugh, you know.'

'So do you think he was involved somehow too? Where would he get that sort of money from? And the Rabbi's organisation. Why them?'

'Daniel, the Rabbi,' she added hastily, 'didn't seem too surprised, but he wouldn't go into it.' She flushed a deep red again and I looked across to the bar at some particularly interesting and neatly stacked bottles.

'And as for Cynthia,' she went on after a moment, 'she either confided her story to George all those years ago or he found out the connection himself. After all, he did have those letters... Either way, he really rained on Claude's parade, didn't he? My God, nobody expected this!' She paused. 'You believe it all now, don't you?'

'I think so,' I said, and explained my conversation with Stephanie.

'Do you think you're – ' she considered her words before continuing – 'over it now. You said you still had a bit of a crush,' she added defensively.

'I don't think I was ever really in it to get over it, if you see what I mean. With Anne leaving so suddenly, I think I just needed *something*. She made me feel...oh, I don't know.' Briefly, memories of Anne touched me. But emotionally I couldn't afford to go down that road again.

We had one more drink and decided to start for home. The weather had worsened, the rush hour was drawing near and AnnaMaria needed to pick up Liam.

I'd had only a bottle and a half of insipid Spanish beer, so I took over the driving after dropping AnnaMaria off at Andy's mum's.

Florence insisted on seeing her new acquisition, despite the hour and the unrelenting storm. We'd had a singsong all the way from Manchester, and I'd spied Flo's hip flask being passed backwards and forwards to her friend.

They were still going strong when I finally pulled into my yard. Spending an afternoon with Florence and Sylvia proved to be more exhausting than an all-night rave in a field in Cheshire. Or a shopping spree with Julia virtually anywhere. I wanted a reviving cup of tea and to put my feet up for an hour. Florence had other ideas.

'Tea? Pah. This is potentially the most exciting thing to happen to me since – ' she considered for a moment – 'my wedding night. And you've no idea what a disappointment that was!'

Mrs Buckham hooted at her companion's acid observation.

'I didn't know you'd been married,' I asked innocently.

'Not for long, I can tell you,' Florence muttered.

'Anyway, forget the kettle, we've got property to investigate,' she insisted. 'Here, have a swig of this instead. Tea! Goodness, woman, live a little,' and she handed me the hip flask.

Clutching the brandy, I stared out of the rain-soaked windscreen at George's (now Florence's) farm. Despite the hour, the sky was almost completely black. The blue of summer had been replaced in a matter of hours by a thoroughly autumnal landscape.

Florence poked me in the back. 'Come on, put this on,' she insisted, and pushed a tiny plastic square into my hands. 'I always carry spares. You never know when you might need them.'

For a sick moment I thought it was a condom and Florence's idea of a joke, but as I unclipped the fastening I saw it was a Rainmate, a waterproof plastic hood designed to cover wedding hats, hairdos and even rollers in inclement weather. Mum used to wear them when I was a kid, but wouldn't thank me for reminding her.

'Come on, put it on,' Flo demanded. 'Nobody will see you out here.'

'Only the hens,' Sylvia cackled. 'Anyway, it's better than catching your death.'

I sighed but pulled the hat over my head. Florence leaned over and tied the ribbon into a neat little bow under my chin. I caught a glimpse of myself in the rear-view mirror. If anybody saw me in this get-up, I'd be single for ever.

I turned to the two women. We were all similarly behatted, one pink, one green, one blue, and we all looked equally ridiculous.

We waited a couple of minutes to see if the rain would lessen, but if anything it became more intense. Under pressure from Flo, we finished off the brandy and ventured into the storm. A blast of air slapped my bonnet against my head. The rain splattered against the pink plastic, the sound of it drumming loudly in my ears.

We squelched through the yard, Mrs Buckham, sensibly dressed in a too long mac, clinging to my arm. 'Have you got a torch?' she bellowed over the wind.

I nodded. 'In the boot. I'll get it.'

The AA-style torch cast a feeble yellowing light. I'd not used it for ages and the batteries were almost flat.

'Won't this keep?' I yelled. 'The house doesn't look very safe.' I stared at the farm, its dark unlived-in presence a precarious blot on the landscape.

'Oh, come on,' Florence said excitedly. 'Nothing keeps at my age, and I've never been one to play it safe,' and with that she pushed me towards the farm.

The dry earth had quickly changed to mud and this made the going difficult. As we skidded across the ground, images of Flo's rickety hips plagued my thoughts. Mrs Buckham, fortified by alcohol, was so close to me she was almost scraping my heel with the toe of her shoe. Lightning suddenly split the sky above us, and the roll of thunder wasn't far behind. I kicked down the dilapidated fencing into Florence's new property and helped the two women climb over. Florence's sudden intake of breath could be heard even over the wind, and the excitement she felt was conveyed to us all.

'Ooh,' Sylvia exclaimed delightedly, and Flo produced the front-door keys from the rain-soaked folder Ruth Smedley had given her.

We didn't need the keys, though. George had never locked his front door in his life. I switched on the torch as the clapped-out door creaked open and we stepped into the kitchen.

Chapter 35

Flo managed to push the door to, effectively shutting out the worsening conditions. The drip, drip of water replaced the steady rumble of the storm.

It was an eerie moment and we were silent as the torchlight picked out the wreckage of Florence's new abode.

'Where's the sink gone?' Mrs Buckham quizzed.

'Where's the bloody floor is more to the point?' Florence snapped as she spotted the great yawning gap where George's floor tiles used to be.

A three-foot ditch appeared in the dim light cast by my torch. Solid wooden planks had been positioned to stop the sides from collapsing. A narrow edge, the remains of terracotta tiles in evidence, had prevented a particularly nasty fall. Somehow I didn't think this was someone's idea of restoring the farm. I had no idea how I'd missed all the activity. Where, for example, was the displaced soil? Where was the machinery used to excavate it? This quarry had not been produced with a spade and trowel.

A sudden chorus of 'The Blue Danube' nearly had us

all leaping into the air and Florence gasped in shock.

'It's all right,' I managed. 'It's just my mobile phone.' With mum's insistence, I'd kept it on my person and I found it deep within my jacket pocket. 'Hello?'

The phone hissed and just as suddenly went dead. The battery warning light had come on and as the connection was lost a muffled crash from upstairs made me drop the phone in shock. Three heads craned upwards.

'I really think we should get out,' I muttered through a dry throat.

'Don't be ridiculous,' Florence said. 'What are you frightened of? Ghosts? It's just the storm, for goodness' sake. Who in their right mind would come visiting this place, in this weather?'

'We have,' I declared.

'It's my new home,' she said simply, then, 'Come on, let's get moving before we all catch pneumonia.' And before I could stop her she snatched the torch from me. 'This way,' she ordered, and, clinging to the kitchen wall, led us gingerly around the room towards the sitting-room door.

I looked towards the ceiling again as we tiptoed across what remained of the floor. Roof supports hung dangerously from the wreckage. It looked as though the bedrooms had been ripped apart as well. I wondered again just how safe this place was.

A sudden desire to escape stopped me in my tracks. Sylvia really did step on my heel then. Florence stalked on ahead and crashed into the adjoining room. We were left alone in the dark, the dripping of water unnaturally loud in the silence.

'What now?' Sylvia asked.

'Florence!' I bellowed as terror crawled up my leg. 'Wait for us.'

There was no reply.

I edged forward. 'Keep to the wall,' I hissed to Sylvia.

'You don't want to fall down there.' A thought occurred to me. 'In fact, you can get out. Here,' I said, my voice squeaky with fear as I fumbled in my jacket for my house keys. 'Go back to my place. Ring...' Ring? Ring who?

'Give Julia a call. Her mobile number is on my pad. Tell her to get over here, quick.'

'If you can't get her, try AnnaMaria. She should be at Andy's mum's.'

'Oh, I know her number. Do you know what she told me in the shop the other day – '

'Sylvia,' I hissed in the dark. 'Please, just go. I want to see where Florence has got to.'

'Oh, okay,' and she turned to leave.

'Watch your step and stick to the wall,' I ordered her retreating back.

'All right, all right, I'm not deaf.'

I waited until I heard the door creak open again. There was a slight shuffle as she let herself out, and rain lashed through the opening.

I turned back to the job at hand, resisting the temptation to follow Sylvia. 'Florence,' I called. 'Wait for me.'

The wall was damp and revolting as I edged my way around the room. It was funny, but the kitchen had never seemed this big when George was alive. Perhaps I'd wandered around it twice. But no, there was the door to the next room. The handle turned easily in my hand and I stepped through into darkness.

A cold draught touched my face, and a strange smell of dampness and something deeply unpleasant drifted into my senses. I couldn't see anything, so sensibly didn't move.

'Florence?' I tried. 'Are you all right?'

Nothing.

The draught suddenly gained intensity and I felt as though someone had stepped past me. I reached out, but only fear touched my fingers.

Gradually, I could make out a shaft of light coming from above. My torch? But it was too strong for that and the colour was wrong. This was a whitish light and I realised, as my eyes became accustomed to its glow, that it was coming through the roof. With so many tiles gone and half the upstairs floor missing, there was enough illumination to make out the dimensions of the room. Rain came in a steady stream through the gaps.

Like the kitchen, this room was in a similarly devastated condition. I looked around, hoping for a sight of Florence, but wherever she was, she wasn't in here.

Another door led, I knew from memory, to the stairs. I checked my footing. The floor to this room too was slowly being deconstructed and, though more of the flooring was still in place, it was clear that, given time, it would end up looking like the kitchen.

With the help of the dim light, I headed for the door. There was no glimmer from the sky to help me here. The stairs were enclosed and I had no idea if I would be able to climb them. A part of me, a huge part of me, was insistent I turn around and go back. But thoughts of Florence lying stricken somewhere drove me on.

The door was slightly ajar and it screeched gently as I opened it. I left it unclosed to let in what light was available. It was precious little, but enough to save me from a fall through missing floorboards. I gingerly stepped over the gap and stretched onto the first stair. The stair rail was gone too, but I couldn't honestly remember whether there had ever been one. With a hand on either side of the walls, I made my way upstairs.

Chapter 36

The miracle was that the stairs were more or less intact. I tripped only once, cracking my knee against uneven and splintered wood. I called Florence's name again, but was answered only by creaking wood and the splash of rain. Finally, after an uncomfortable count of thirteen steps, I faced the bedroom door. I pushed it and it swung open on rusty hinges, elderly wood rubbing against metal, and then I saw Florence, looking pale and dazed and sprawled in a corner.

After all the care I'd taken getting into the damn place, you'd think I would have been equally cautious approaching the old woman. But I rushed towards her and a hard, powerful hand slapped me full in the chest. Winded, I flew backwards through the doorway I'd just entered and landed with a thud across the loose boards.

I didn't even have a chance to check if I'd been injured or take a breath to scream before the hand buried itself in my hair and dragged me back into the bedroom. I suddenly found myself face-down looking through a gap, a fifteen-foot drop between me and the room below.

I managed a scream then. But only a short one, as a knee landed heavily on my back. Ribs groaned under the pressure and I had hardly enough air to breathe now, much less scream. Breath of another sort suddenly hissed in my ear. 'Give me your hand, bitch,' a male voice ordered. Expensive aftershave mixed with the smell I'd tried to identify. The smell of sewers, I realised, drifting up from ruptured pipes.

But bitch? Nobody had ever said that to me, at least not to my face. The hand twisted in my hair. If I got out of this, I'd have the lot cut off, I thought hysterically.

His knee eased from my back and I was hauled to a sitting position. He stuck a finger in my face. What next? Poke my eye out? I didn't even know what I was going to do until I did it.

Grabbing his finger, I bent it backwards as hard as I could. It was amazingly effective, and as his hand loosened its grip on my hair I hauled myself to my knees. Gasping with a combination of pain and terror, I scrabbled across the floor on all fours. Completely disoriented, I was pulled up by a familiar voice.

'Letty, just stop,' Stephanie said from the shadows.

I collapsed then, as effectively as if someone had shot me.

Footsteps creaked across the floor and Stephanie knelt beside me. 'Show me your hand,' she demanded quietly. 'He'll hurt you again if you don't.'

'What did I ever do to you?' I gasped.

'Nothing.' She smiled sadly. 'Nothing at all.'

And Stephanie gently prised my hand open. Her husband, breathless and angry, shone a bright light on my upturned palm.

'The bathroom,' Stephanie muttered. 'Christ, how did we miss it? It's in the bathroom, the only place we haven't looked.' She let my hand go and it fell, unfeeling, across my chest. A huge flash of lightning threw the room into clear view and suddenly more roof tiles were dislodged, crashing to the floor and shattering around me. Sharp pieces of clay stung exposed flesh. Florence stirred in the corner. Muttering to herself in what sounded suspiciously like Italian, she dragged herself to a sitting position.

'Letty,' she called from across the room, 'are you all right?'

'Never felt better,' and I giggled hysterically.

'Where are they?' She asked her surprising question in a surprisingly strong voice.

'Bathroom,' I said as sounds of destruction engulfed the racket caused by the storm. I didn't trust myself, or my voice, with further explanations.

'Get up, Letty, and get out. Now!' she ordered. 'What a fool I am,' she admonished herself. 'I should have known they'd be here. Pride, that's all it is. I'm as guilty as the rest. I thought I could do what was so easy thirty, forty years ago. Foolish old woman,' and she burst into tears.

That, more than anything, had me moving across the room. I gave the hole in the floor a wide berth and went to hold Florence. She was muttering in Italian again, and a name was repeated several times through her sobs.

'Cynthia,' she said over and over again. 'My love, I need you now,' she said in English.

It was suddenly obvious why the face in the old black and white photo had seemed so familiar.

'Florence, ssh. Please, listen to me.'

'I'm not Florence,' she whispered.

'I know. I know who you are. Imrie, come on, let's get out of here.'

Chapter 37

She didn't scream when I picked her up, so I assumed all her bones were as they should be. The floor was even more treacherous and I really couldn't see how I'd get her downstairs, or even beyond the bathroom without being noticed. But in the end I didn't have to worry about that. Above the racket of the storm and my companion's steady stream of Italian, I heard a car roaring down the driveway. Curses floated from the bathroom and above it all I heard Stephanie shout, 'Come on! Leave it, just leave it,' and the clatter of footsteps as they hurtled down the stairs.

I edged past the bathroom door and peered in to make sure they really had gone. The side of the government-installed bath had been ripped apart, a steady stream of water gushed from the smashed pipes and the decorated plastic side-panel lay across the floor. Could there really have been anything of value hidden in such a small space?

I adjusted my grip on the older woman. She was almost weightless but not as fragile as I'd first thought. I realised, as I gazed at the bath, that the pattern across the panel was nauseatingly familiar.

My hand held the same marks. A similar design had been painted on the kitchen floor too, I realised, thinking back to George's remembrance service.

Fired by a need to make some sense of it all, I propped the older woman at the top of the stairs. A good gust of wind and she'd go tumbling down, so I made her sit on the top step. She was crying again and I patted her bony arm.

'I won't be a minute,' I promised, and I crept gingerly into the bathroom. Lightning crackled again and the thunder that followed was barely a second behind. The tatty rug was sodden and the floorboards beneath it were dangerously soft. There was at least a two-inch play before it decided to hold my weight.

I knelt down and peered into the recess beneath the side of the bath. Whatever Claude and Stephanie had been after was still there and something glinted in the half-light.

Water gushed ever more powerfully from broken pipes and pouring rain. The bath, dislodged from its moorings, was slightly tilted to face me and I reached underneath it tentatively, hoping to get a grip on the object I'd spotted.

It was surprisingly dry. Water hadn't found its way into the bath's recesses. I leaned in as far as I could and scrabbled about, touching something solid and heavy. My heart beat that little bit faster and, holding on for a better grip, I yanked as hard as I could. The object moved, but so did the bath. I felt the floorboards shift under my feet. Water streamed over the sides of the bath, over my shoes, down my trousers – an icy flow that wrenched the breath from my lungs.

I tried to struggle to my feet, but at that moment the floorboards and the rotten carpet succumbed to the sudden assault and the ground literally opened beneath me. Wood creaked and splintered, its sharp edges raking my body as I plunged through the collapsing floor. I clung to the as-yet-undisclosed object and it jammed somehow under the bath. I held on with one arm, water cascading around my head from ruptured pipes and my legs dangled through the ceiling of the kitchen directly below.

The bath creaked ominously above my head. If the pipes holding it in place gave way... well, basically I was fucked.

I tried not to think about my arm. I'm not a weak person but there was only so much strain my muscles could take. Already they were quivering with the effort of clinging on. Actually, my whole body was quivering. Florence's bloody plastic hat wasn't helping matters. It had crept over my forehead, its sharp edges digging painfully into my eyes. My arm was going numb and I was slowly being blinded. I screeched for help. The bath shifted position and more water flooded over me.

I tried to haul myself up, but I couldn't get a purchase with my free hand and I knew, as pain shot through my tendons, that my right arm couldn't hold my weight much longer. I didn't know how far I would fall before hitting the kitchen floor but even a six-foot drop would be more than enough to cause serious bodily damage, especially with an Armitage Shanks vitreous enamel bath complete with chrome accessories crashing down on top of me.

A hand suddenly stretched through the gap between myself, the floorboards and the bath. An old hand, wrinkled but surprisingly firm, gripped my collar. It was all I needed and, grappling for anything of substance, my left hand happened upon one of the chrome bath taps. With Florence's encouragement I managed to haul myself up through the gap in the floor. The object I'd clung to finally came free and, as I staggered out of the bathroom onto firmer ground, the bath finally slithered through the hole I'd just vacated, taking with it ageing pipes and plumbing paraphernalia that crashed to the kitchen floor beneath. It sounded like a bomb going off.

I grabbed the older woman and hauled her into my arms with what little strength I had left. We had to get out before the whole damned house collapsed around us.

Shoving the mystery object into her hands, I took the first tentative step on the stairway. It creaked ominously beneath my feet. Holding my breath, I took the next one. The creaks got worse.

'Go down on your own,' Imrie whispered in my ear. 'We're too heavy together.'

'Please,' I gasped. 'What do you weigh? Six stone?'

'I used to be so strong,' she murmured.

'Well,' I replied, peering into the gloom below. Tentatively I tested the next step with one foot. 'I hope I'm in the same shape you are when I'm your age.'

'Don't be patronising,' she scolded.

Laughter seemed inappropriate but it couldn't be stopped. And that's how AnnaMaria found us, the pair of us giggling away on steps about to collapse, one foot waving ineffectually in the air.

'AnnaMaria?' I asked, and the laughter faded away.

'It's all right,' Imrie whispered in my ear. 'AnnaMaria, help us,' she said.

'I've got you,' she said gently, and she leaned towards the old woman, tendering younger, stronger arms, and relieving me of her weight. 'Come on,' she said.

I sat down with a thud and didn't move again until a few minutes later, when AnnaMaria came back for me. I looked at her blankly.

'You'll have to help me. I can't carry you,' she coaxed. 'Come on, Letty. You're not hurt, are you? And what in God's name are you wearing?'

I remembered my hat but was too exhausted to bother taking it off.

'There's never a camera when you need one,' she said, reaching for me.

I leaned against her and she led me downstairs and out of the house.

The fierce storm had retreated to a summer shower and, as the setting sun struggled against the thinning clouds, a rainbow materialised in the distance. If a choir of angels had appeared, I'd have gone back in the house and taken my chances.

What I had expected to see wasn't there at all. No police cars, no ambulances, no local bobby saving the day. Just Sylvia flapping about counselling Florence, Imrie, whoever, on the doorstep of George's old farm.

'Where is everybody?' I asked AnnaMaria.

'Who were you expecting?' she responded with a smile.

'I don't know,' I admitted. 'The police, for example?'

'It'll keep,' she said. 'Come on,' and, smiling, she pulled my plastic cap from my head. 'Let's get you home.'

Chapter 38

A wide-eyed Julia arrived just as Sylvia and AnnaMaria began arguing about how to make the perfect cup of tea. I'd taken Florence upstairs and ordered her skinny, wrinkly and bruised but otherwise unhurt body into the bath.

'AnnaMaria's rung the doctor,' I said, turning my back. 'And she'll contact the police, I suppose.' Whatever Claude and Stephanie had been up to, they were guilty of assault if nothing else.

'Later, Letty,' Imrie insisted as she eased herself into the suds. 'And don't be so prudish,' she laughed quakily. 'Women have seen me naked before, you know.'

I blushed. 'Yes, but not this one.'

Her laughter got stronger. 'I want to explain some things to you first,' she decided, her Florence persona to the fore. She sighed. 'This bath is wonderful. Come on, Letty,' she coaxed. 'Come and listen to me. I can't talk to your back all night.'

Overcoming my own embarrassment, I sat on the downturned loo seat and gave her my full attention.

*

The bath had been topped up with warm water several times by the end of Imrie's story.

'So you see, Cynthia and I . . .' she paused. 'We were perfect together, though we had so little time. I had every intention of coming back to her, you know. But once I'd returned to Prague to visit my mother I found it impossible to leave again. The doors were effectively locked to me. Sounds silly doesn't it? And I don't expect you to understand. Not properly.'

She smiled at me and a pair of bony hands reached over the side of the bath for a towel.

'So when did you return to England? And how are you really related to George Evershaw? *Are* you related?'

'Distantly. My marriage was a short one and I only did it as a way of getting to England. Marriages of convenience weren't recently invented,' she said, and I suddenly thought of Stephanie and Claude, but I let her comment pass. 'Cynthia was already dead by the time I got here. So sad. I miss her so much,' and she mumbled something in Italian.

'Mum's story was accurate enough then?'

'Spot on,' Imrie agreed.

Neither of us said anything for a while.

'What about that piece of metal I found under the bath?' I ventured finally.

Heavy and made of brass with a strange silver trim, its abstract shape gave no clue, to me at any rate, as to its origin.

'It's a piece of sculpture,' Imrie explained, drying her face.

'Modern art of the Twenties. Invaluable to some, and it saved your life,' she added with a grin.

'Imrie, you saved my life,' I said, reaching for her hand. 'Do you think any of the other artworks survived then?' I asked after a while.

'Oh, they'll be somewhere. I knew Rabbi Burns' family,

you know. Art dealers the lot of them, and Czech Jews too, despite the name. And from what I know of him, if anybody can track them down, he can. It's not surprising George had so much money to leave. He must have sold the lot. Didn't spend all the money, though.'

'I wonder why?'

She looked at me. 'Guilt? Cynthia will have threatened him. I can almost hear her. "Sell it, and I'll haunt you".' She gave an eerie impression of my long-dead aunt. 'Come on,' she said. 'Help me out of here. I can't afford to get any more wrinkly than I already am.'

I hauled her out, patted her dry and headed out of the bathroom in search of dry clothes.

I walked straight into Sylvia, her ear glued to the door. Flustered, she said, 'The doctor's here.'

'Send him up,' Imrie called from the bathroom. 'I'm going for a lie-down, if that's all right, Letty?'

'No problem,' I called back and described the whereabouts of my bedroom. 'And it's a "her",' I advised.

'Sylvia," Imrie commanded, "come and keep me company. I've got some explaining to do to you too.'

Chapter 39

'I can't understand why she didn't leave the stuff with Mum,' I asked as the doctor examined Imrie.

'Oh, Letty, you know what your mother's like. She would have been down to the police and lost property before you could blink. Too honest sometimes, that one,' AnnaMaria pointed out.

'Have you rung her?' I asked.

'No,' AnnaMaria said hastily. 'I thought I'd leave that to you. Though, somehow, I don't think she'll have much of a problem believing it, do you?'

I shook my head as Julia brought more tea over. 'And that's all you don't understand?' she asked. 'Well, you're doing better than me then.'

I didn't bother with an answer.

'You ought to see the doc as well, you know,' she suggested.

'Don't worry about me, Julia. I'm just a bit stiff.' I sighed.

The doctor reappeared then and she looked at our group suspiciously. 'What's been going on here then? Your friend upstairs isn't giving much away,' she said. 'I hope you've rung the police. If you haven't, I'm going to report it myself.'

Dr Weiss had never been a woman to mince her words and I'd always found her a bit scary. She knew her stuff though.

'Letty, get on the couch. I want to have a look at you. Everybody else, out you go.'

She looked in my eyes, lifting first one eyelid, then the other. She smelled of soap.

'How do you feel?' the doctor asked.

'A bit scratched and a bit winded, that's all. Except my arm aches. I think I've pulled a muscle.'

Dislocated my shoulder, more like. And suddenly I wanted to tell this mother figure every medical problem I'd ever had, or had ever been scared of, since I was six years old. She had that kind of face.

'Let's have a look, shall we?' she asked as doctors do, and, smiling, she gave me her full attention as she proceeded to check my vital signs.

Eventually I was pronounced fit.

'Are you going to tell me then?' she asked. 'I meant what I said, you know.'

I thought for a minute as I pulled my shirt back on. 'I'll ring the police. I'd better explain to them.'

She smiled. 'Wise move, Letty,' and then she packed her stuff together, gave me a prescription for Imrie and left.

Sergeant Sam was reduced to scratching his head with a pencil when, hours later, with input from AnnaMaria, I told him the whole story.

'I'm going to have to pass this on. I think you can expect a visit from CID,' he informed me gruffly. 'I don't know how you get involved in stuff like this. You never learn, do you?'

I didn't need his observations, no matter how accurate they were.

'And get your mother down here too with those letters. My guess is that all this is going to throw some light on George Evershaw's death. It'll hold the inquest up even longer. But that's not really for me to decide and, as far as you're concerned, I never said that.'

True to Sam's word, the whole of the British police force were down on us like a ton of bricks. But he was wrong about George Evershaw's inquest. The findings were made public within a couple of weeks, weeks I'd spent telling the same story to anyone who asked. I was sick of hearing my own voice, as was Imrie, whose life story was suddenly public property.

She wasn't pleased. And neither was Claude Adam, dragged in for questioning over George's death but eventually, with no evidence against him, charged only with assault, though Imrie, like me, has decided not to press charges.

Julia can't understand why, though Mum could empathise with our reasoning. Enough was enough as far as I was concerned.

And George Evershaw? A close call between accidental death and an open verdict. The open verdict won out.

A Calderton resident resolved one question during the hearing, as to why my neighbour should have dead rabbits in the bathroom and a tub full of water. George's habit was to clear his illegal snares, littered around the area, mid-evening. The bathwater was used to clean the carcasses. Mrs Buckham's observations that the room was awash with blood proved to be accurate, though not much of it belonged to George, after all.

Janice's tacky headline that night read: 'NEIGHBOUR ASKS, WAS HE PUSHED OR DID HE FALL?'

I had no idea how she got away with it.

Chapter 40

And after that nobody really told me much more. Except Imrie, who, despite years spent keeping secrets, made a confession of sorts to me one quiet and warm sunny afternoon. But all she really wanted to do was live out the rest of her days in Calderton as peacefully as possible.

Her farm was uninhabitable and she really couldn't be bothered with the palaver of having it knocked down only to be rebuilt again. 'It can fall down for all I care,' she said adjusting the lounger. Strangers in dark suits had bustled about the place, looking for God-knows-what for a couple of days, but had left empty-handed. AnnaMaria had told me that the Rabbi had flown off to Tel Aviv with the money destined for his peace organisation. The whole thing was too unbelievable to even question.

Imrie eased back in the sunshine with a sigh. 'No, Sylvia said I can stay with her as long as I want, and I probably will now. I'm close to Cynthia's resting place and I can come and see you whenever I want. That is all right, isn't it?' she asked me a little anxiously, looking every day of her eighty-two years.

I smiled at her. 'Visit whenever you want to. Except there is one thing I'd like you to explain.'

'What's that?' she asked politely.

'Water wells?'

She laughed. 'I had to tell Sylvia something, didn't I? She's like you. You don't believe the truth until it's in your face.'

We sat together in the sunshine that afternoon and she told me of her past life; Cynthia's story from another angle. She laughed when I expressed concern at the marks on my hand. 'Just another one of our little games. Remind me to read those letters to you some time. It was strange to see my own words again after all these years.'

Imrie did tell me of her life's great tragedies, though she dwelt on the greater joys, and as she talked and described and sometimes tried to justify herself, I didn't interrupt.

It was quite the saddest story I had ever heard. But sometimes, just sometimes, I got a glimpse of the woman Cynthia had fallen in love with. Beneath the person Imrie wanted us all to see was another woman altogether. And I began to understand.

Hours later, exhausted and emotional, she fell asleep. We never talked of it again.

Sita came to see me the following week. The discovery (or lack of discovery) of the hidden art had dismayed her, her recent Parliamentary work having been a curious coincidence. She was, however, offered the diplomatic job of returning the one surviving piece of sculpture to the Kinsky Museum in Prague. Julia was itching to go with her.

Mum paid several calls and spent one particularly long, hot afternoon with Imrie. I knew tears were shed and private thoughts shared. Funnily enough, my mother's relationship with me, and mine with her, suddenly improved. We were never going to be as close as perhaps we'd like, but somehow a barrier between us collapsed.

Sadly, Imrie died a few months later, peacefully, as she'd hoped, in her sleep. And when she died, the secrets of this particular *Girl's Own* adventure died with her. Mum swore she'd never mention it again. Not to me, not to her brother, who'd been approached and questioned by the FBI, not to anyone.

Though a headlining story in the *Calderton Echo*, it had only just scraped into the nationals. Understandably, the inhabitants of the village have talked of nothing else for months.

We buried Imrie next to Cynthia in the local cemetery. It was a quiet, sad affair, a couple of black-suited strangers adding to the slightly unreal feeling of the occasion.

Rabbi Burns, a nonconformist himself apparently, had returned from Tel Aviv to hold a joint service for Imrie with the local Methodist minister. It was a long, cold and sad day. But, like the old verse, we planted a red rose on one grave and a briar on the other.

Mum and Sylvia cried for hours.

I got her farm. Suddenly I was potentially the richest person I knew. I had no idea what I'd do with the place. It was fenced off now – the building was far too dangerous to go near. I supposed it was down to me to make it safe.

I got one unexpected call. Anne, having read the story and heard further rumours from the village's rumour factory, wondering how life was treating me. Better without you, my own personal devil wanted to say, but I was polite and guarded and cold. The call lasted all of fifteen seconds.

The final word had to be Julia's.

One evening, baby-sitting for AnnaMaria, the phone

interrupted the spy film I was engrossed in, though it was a little tame to be honest. I debated whether to answer it or not, but didn't want to miss a call from Spielberg, should he want to buy the film rights to Cynthia's story.

It was Julia, of course.

'Listen, I've had this fantastic idea.'

'I don't care,' I interrupted.

'Yeah, but there's this woman I know. She's got some friends who are interested in developing a holiday centre. Jacuzzis, spas, mineral baths, massages, aromatherapy. The whole enchillada.'

'Julia . . .'

They're offering a fantastic price.'

'Julia . . .'

'They're willing to rent.'

'Julia . . .'

You can't lose.'

'Julia . . .'

'Look, I'll leave it with you, okay?'

'JULIA!' I bellowed. 'JULIA, I'M NOT PLAYING ANY MORE.'

But it was no good. She'd already hung up.

Alma Fritchley
Chicken Feed
The second Letty Campbell mystery

When Letty's lover Anne sets off for a US-wide lecture tour,
Letty prepares for a mournful few weeks alone on the farm
with only her chickens for company. But her peace is shattered
by the arrival of a strange woman in her kitchen with a wild and
appealing five-year-old child. Before she knows it, their troubles
are hers and Letty is caught up in a sequence of rapid, outrageous
and dangerous events. Why has charismatic lesbian politician Sita
Joshi suddenly disappeared? How come Letty's gorgeous ex-lover
Julia has wound up in jail? What has it got to do with the top
lesbian singer recently in town? And what is on the video tape
that turns up in the village and almost costs Letty her life . . . ?

'A terrific yarn . . . mightily recommended.' *Diva*

'This book had me laughing out loud.' *Crime Time*

Crime Fiction £6.99
ISBN 0 7043 4570 6

Also of interest:

Alma Fritchley
Chicken Run
The first Letty Campbell mystery

'Julia was watching me carefully. "Well?" I said, "What
gives?" Before she could answer, the inner sanctum of
Steigel Senior's office was revealed and Steigel Senior
herself appeared in the doorway. Julia leapt to her feet
and in that sudden movement all was revealed. Julia was
wonderfully, newly, ecstatically in love, probably truly for
the first time in her life, and who could blame her?
Steigel Senior was a cool-eyed, blond-haired Lauren
Bacall, complete with Dietrich's mystery and Garbo's
gorgeous accent ... '

When Letty Campbell warily agrees to let her land be used for
a classic car auction, she has no idea what lies ahead. Why is her
gorgeous ex, Julia, really so desperate for the auction to happen?
Is the new love of Julia's life as suspicious as she seems? And why
does Letty have a horrible feeling that she should never have
got involved?

'Hilarious.' *Evening Standard*

'Irrepressibly bouncy.' *Pink Paper*

'A breath of fresh air ... Alma Fritchley is a talent
to watch.' *Crime Time*

Crime Fiction £6.99
ISBN 0 7043 4515 3